Showdown
with the Sheriff

JAN HAMBRIGHT

MILLS & BOON®

Pure reading pleasure™

First published in Great Britain 2008
by Harlequin Mills & Boon Limited,
Eton House, 18-24 Paradise Road, Richmond, Surrey TW9 1SR

© M Jan Hambright 2007

ISBN: 978 0 263 85985 0

46-0808

Harlequin Mills & Boon policy is to use papers that are natural, renewable and recyclable products and made from wood grown in sustainable forests. The logging and manufacturing processes conform to the legal environmental regulations of the country of origin.

Printed and bound in Spain
by Litografía Rosés S.A., Barcelona

To my dad. Thanks for keeping the faith and being my number one fan. Love ya, always.

ABOUT THE AUTHOR

Jan Hambright penned her first novel at seventeen, but claims it was pure rubbish. However, it did open the door on her love for storytelling. Born in Idaho, she resides there with her husband, three of their five children, a three-legged watchdog and a spoiled horse named Texas, who always has time to listen to her next story idea while they gallop along.

A self-described adrenaline junkie, Jan spent ten years as a volunteer EMT in rural Idaho, and jumped out of an aeroplane at ten thousand feet attached to a man with a parachute, just to celebrate turning forty. Now she hopes to make your adrenaline level rise along with that of her danger-seeking characters. She would like to hear from her readers and hopes you enjoy the story world she has created for you. Jan can be reached at PO Box 2537, McCall, Idaho 83638, USA.

CAST OF CHARACTERS

Logan Brewer – The Belle County Sheriff was just a deputy when Rory Matson was abducted and left for dead on Reaper's Point. Can he overcome the guilt he harbours for not saving her the first time, and catch the killer before his rage turns to obsession?

Aurora (Rory) Matson – She ran away from Reaper's Point after her near-death experience. But when her father is murdered, she's forced to return and face her fears.

Doctor Matson – He never gave up on finding his daughter's abductor. He hiked the mountain in a relentless search until the day he was murdered. Will his gruesome discovery ever be revealed?

Deputy Wade Sparks – The boy next door, with a friendly smile and a ready hand. Could he be the killer's next target?

Deputy Taylor – After reckless handling of evidence that cost the department a conviction last time – will he pull it all together for this case?

Brady Morris – An over-privileged and arrogant search-and-rescue worker who has secrets he's not sharing.

Chapter One

Aurora Matson shoved a cookbook into the over-stuffed box on the kitchen counter and dusted off her hands. Cleaning out her father's cabin didn't feel right. But neither did the fact that he was dead.

A climbing accident, the local sheriff's office had said, but she couldn't get her head around details that were totally uncharacteristic of her dad. He'd always been meticulous when it came to safety.

But even that inconsistency in character couldn't change the fact that he was gone and she was alone. Back in Reaper's Point, the exact place she'd sworn she'd never return to.

She swallowed against the tightness in her throat and sat down on a stool at the counter.

Two weeks. She could do two weeks here. The arrangements would be taken care of by then, the date set for the memorial, his cabin cleared of personal items. And she'd be free to return to Los Angeles and her job as a forensic-reconstruction artist, building faces where none exist.

The lab had been in the middle of a baffling case when the call about her dad came in. The sooner she returned, the sooner she could help the police catch a sadistic killer who'd murdered two girls.

The last of the evening sun dipped behind a bank of ponderosa pine in a burst of coral and deep purple. She'd loved this mountain once. Soaked it into her soul every chance she'd had. Climbing it had been her passion, its pull greater than anything she'd ever experienced.

Tears stung the back of her eyelids as she thought of her father. He'd become another victim of Reaper's Point. But at least he'd died doing something he'd loved.

The low hum of an engine rumbling down the narrow driveway into the cabin site interrupted her tangled thoughts and kept her from collapsing into a heap on the floor.

The decisive tromp of boots against deck board sent a shiver through her.

Glancing out the kitchen window she spotted the police vehicle parked in the drive and relaxed. It was a formality. A minor moment in time when her father's personal effects would be returned to her. A moment when it would all become as real as the fingers on her hands or the ache in her heart.

She strode to the front door, suddenly hungry for the company of another human being. A voice to fill the haunting stillness that surrounded her like thick fog.

Turning the knob, she pulled open the door and stared up at Belle County Sheriff Logan Brewer, his face shielded under the brim of a dove-gray Stetson.

Her nerves tightened as a flood of memories washed over her, rippling a familiar pool of desire inside her body.

"Aurora. Have you got a minute?"

Caught between curiosity and dread, she stepped back and let him enter, catching a whiff of his spicy aftershave as it trailed in with him on the early evening air.

"Sure. I assume you're here to return my father's things?"

He paused in the middle of the living room, filling the area with his presence.

She couldn't keep her gaze off the broad expanse of his shoulders inside his uniform or the easy way he took up space as though he owned it. There was no denying he'd grown up and muscled out in all the right places since the summer they'd spent together.

She fought to douse the burst of heat flaming inside her, burning her cheeks. He was the same as he'd been all those years ago. The man whose department had stamped Cold Case on her file—and her life.

He pulled off his hat and turned toward her.

Rory's breath caught as she stared into his dark

brown eyes, which were intent and focused on her alone. There was a hard set to his square jaw and she instantly wanted to smooth her hand against his face.

"I didn't come to return his things. We found something in his backpack the day we recovered his body."

"And?" She tried to repel the images his admission put into her head.

"I'd like you to take a look."

An ounce of bitterness spilled from inside her and spread, washing away any decorum she had left. "You're kidding, right?"

His body visibly tensed. He curled the brim of the hat he held in his hands. "Look, Rory."

"Please. Call me Aurora." It took every ounce of restraint she had not to come apart.

He nodded, maybe understanding there no longer existed anything between them. "Your dad found something on Reaper's Point. Something that may have contributed to his death."

"I knew it. I knew he wouldn't have made an amateur mistake like neglecting to tie off. He was seasoned. It makes no sense." A mix of relief and horror coursed through her.

"I'd like you to come down to the station. My department's strapped—maybe you'd consider working your magic on the evidence he had in his possession at the time of his death."

"Human remains?" The blood left her face and pooled in her feet.

"A partial skull, wrapped in a towel at the bottom of his pack. There's no way to make an identification without a full reconstruction. The lower jawbone is missing, along with the teeth."

She sucked in a breath and looked away. "There are outside labs. I'm here to bury my father."

"I want you. You're the best."

She looked up and saw a brief smile turn his lips before it disappeared back into his rugged features. She wanted to throw his arrogance back at him, but a zing of pride shot through her. "I'll need a kit and software."

"Anything you want, it's yours."

She could live with that, but what she didn't like was her body's primal response to the pleased grin on his mouth. A mouth she'd kissed more times than she could recount and always with the same result. Total annihilation of her senses.

"I'll get my jacket and lock up." The thought of having something to do, of not being in the cabin alone for another evening, was somehow comforting, she thought as she climbed into the Blazer with Logan. But she couldn't shake the uneasy sensation creeping through her.

Reaper's Point rarely gave up its dead—or its secrets—without a fight.

LOGAN WATCHED RORY cradle the human skull in her gloved hands like an adoring lover. He looked away, bothered by the streak of resignation riding over his nerves. He'd had his chance and he'd made a mess of it.

"Female. I'll need to take precise measurements and feed them into the computer before I'm absolutely sure, but I'd say Caucasian, early to mid-twenties. She's been on the mountain for a long time. I'd guess three to four years, judging by the breakdown of the bone and weathering."

"I'm impressed." He was impressed. Impressed with her. The girl he'd fallen for more than six years ago had turned into a woman. From her shoulder-length dark blond hair to the delicious curves of her body, he memorized every aspect.

"Don't be. My father could have told you the same thing, and probably would have if he'd made it off the mountain alive."

"I'm sorry, Rory." This time she didn't scold him, didn't try to remove the nickname from his vocabulary as if the intimacy they'd once shared had never existed. He was grateful for that. His body responded to the memories, but he tamped them down.

"All I want is to know what really happened up there."

"And I'm going to find out. I promise." He moved toward her, but stopped short. He'd promised her things before. Promises he wasn't able to keep.

The air in the room crackled with pent-up

energy. Their gazes locked over the desk as she carefully set the skull down.

"It's late. I need to get a call out to my lab. They can overnight supplies. I should be able to give her a face before Dad's memorial service."

"I know this is hard for you." He stepped closer, feeling an invisible barrier go up between them. Hell, he'd thought he was past it, but seeing her again was like pouring gasoline on smoldering embers.

"I'd like you to take a look at the scene."

She turned watery green eyes on him, but behind the veiled tears he saw determination. "Where?"

"The north face. Tip of the point."

The air pushed out of Rory's lungs. She sucked in a deep breath to replace it. Dormant fear awakened in her with a vengeance as she stared into his face. "I—I don't think I can go up there."

He stepped toward her, reaching out, he clasped her forearms.

Heat shot through her, burning where they made contact.

"I'm sorry. I have no right to ask, I just thought you might catch something we may have missed…."

"I'll go." The words were out before she could pull them back. Her knees started to buckle. Only Logan's steady hands on her arms kept her from a total meltdown as images from the past flashed in her mind.

"I'll be with you every step of the way." There

was comfort in his words, but it was quickly re-placed by her own doubts.

"I'm going to need a weapon. I can't go up there unarmed."

A knowing look creased his brows together. "If it'll make you feel safer, I've got an extra service revolver. Will that do?"

"Yeah." She suddenly felt defeated. Pulling out of his grasp, she leaned against the edge of the desk.

He was too close. Too entwined with her reasons for leaving Reaper's Point. "I'll make that call and you can take me home."

"Sure." He lifted the phone receiver from its cradle and handed it to her. She rattled off the num-ber and he punched it in.

"L.A. Crime Lab. How may I direct your call?"

"Jonas MacCafferty, please."

"One moment."

Rory waited for the call to go through, studying Logan in the interim. They were the same age, thirty-one, but she'd outgrown him the summer she turned twenty-five. Something about near-death experiences puts life in prospective.

"Hello?"

"Jonas, glad I caught you."

"How are you?"

"Surviving. But I may need a couple of extra days here."

"Everything all right?"

"Yeah." Her stomach knotted as the reply left her mouth. Things weren't all right. There was tension in the air. Tension and uneasiness had settled into her bones the moment she'd learned about the skull.

"I need a favor. I need a total reconstruct kit overnighted along with the measurement software. Can you handle it?"

"No problem, but what's the deal. Are you moonlighting?"

"No. There's been an interesting find here and an old friend needs my help." She glanced at Logan, watched the muscle along his jaw pulse. They'd been so much more than friends.

She turned away from him, needing distance from the ebb and flow of emotion boiling inside of her. She had to help figure out what her dad was doing with a skull in his pack, where he'd gotten it and who it belonged to. She couldn't walk away.

"Where shall I send it?"

"Belle County Sheriff's Department. In care of Sheriff Logan Brewer."

"Logan…Logan…isn't he the guy who dropped the ball in your…"

"Yes." She was glad Jonas took the hint and didn't try to finish his sentence. She'd finished it a million times in her own head, but now wasn't the time. Right now she needed to focus on her father's suspicious death.

"Thanks. I owe you."

"I think lunch at Ronaldo's should cover it."

"Ronaldo's it is."

"If you get in a spot up there, let me know. I'd love to take some vacation time. Hike around on the mountain, enjoy the fall colors."

"I will. See ya." The phone went dead in her hand. She turned around and hung up.

Logan had taken a seat in the oversized leather chair behind the desk and was looking content.

An old ache festered in her chest as the memory of his hands on her body floated to the surface of her mind. They'd had something special before a madman had taken it away. Logan had been a deputy back then. Green as a willow in spring.

Anger and regret swamped the melancholy thoughts and her heart hardened—a happening she'd been less able to control for the last six years.

"The kit will be here tomorrow. I'll spend a couple of days on the restoration. You should be able to get her picture out to the media by week's end."

He rocked forward in his chair. "Thanks. So are you up for a hike tomorrow morning?"

"What time?" Fear leached into her body.

"Nine o'clock. That should give us plenty of daylight. Tomorrow there should be excellent conditions." He stood up and came around the desk. "I should get you home."

Instinctively, she sidestepped him, avoiding another contact. She couldn't risk having him touch her, no matter how innocently. Better to keep the wall up.

"This Jonas character, he a friend of yours?"

She followed along behind him as they exited his office.

"A colleague."

"I see."

"He offered to come up for a few days if we need him."

"That won't be necessary. I know you can handle it." He stopped next to a large gun safe. He spun the combination lock before grasping the handle and pulling it open. "Do you need a holster?"

Preoccupied, she stared at the arsenal inside the safe.

"Will you be shoving it in your waistband, then?" His voice was heavy with humor.

"This isn't a cop show. I'll take the holster and the gun. I'm not going up there without it."

He sobered, staring at her long and hard before lifting down a dark brown leather holster. "Have you got a belt?"

"Yeah. I'll use one of Dad's if I have to."

"Probably not thick enough. Try this one."

He took out a three-inch-wide belt designed for carrying a weapons holster.

"You can't have a pistol flopping around while you hike. I like my ears—and my life." He grinned, showing even white teeth. But it was the wink he gave her that forced her heartbeat up a notch.

And he did have great ears. Ears she'd nibbled at and whispered into in the middle of the night....

"I'm going to have one of my deputies come along."

"Okay." Before she could protest he had the belt around her waist.

He worked the buckle, cinching it up tight.

The close contact put her on edge. The scent of aftershave warmed by his body wafted into her nose, bombarding her senses with desire.

She took a step back to avoid being pulled into the intoxicating sensation.

"Feels comfortable. It'll do."

Logan took a shiny stub-nose .38 out of the safe and shoved it into the holster.

Anxious to leave, Rory whirled around almost slamming into a young deputy who'd appeared out of nowhere.

"Whoa." He caught her by the shoulders, steadied and released her.

"You must be Dr. Matson's daughter? I'm Deputy Sparks. I'm sure sorry about your old man."

"Thank you." She liked Sparks. His easy demeanor had a calming effect on her shattered nerves.

"She has agreed to go up the mountain with us tomorrow. We're going to have another look at the crime scene."

She turned on Logan, angered by his lack of candor. "Crime scene? You mean there's straightforward evidence?"

Logan stepped toward her, irritated with himself

for not giving her all of the information. Maybe he should have trusted her. Maybe she had gotten over the past. Hell, maybe he was just being stubborn. She'd always accused him of being stubborn.

"Look, Rory. I didn't want to dump this on you. I didn't want you to feel uncomfortable here. I know how hard it was for you to come back to Reaper's Point. So I'll give it to you straight. The coroner's report indicates he was dead before he plunged off the north face. There was blunt-force trauma to his head that didn't line up with the damage on his helmet."

Her expression turned to horror, then fluctuated between disbelief and anger. "When were you going to tell me?"

"I wasn't holding out on you. I just wanted to be sure you were…able to handle it."

She straightened like a soldier coming to attention. It was as if she'd encased herself in steel. He didn't know whether to be glad or on guard.

"I'm not twenty-five, anymore. There's not a maniac on the mountain trying to kill me. I want in on this investigation."

Concern bristled his nerves. Was she strong enough to withstand whatever they might find? Even steel had a melting point.

"Okay. You're in."

"Glad you see it my way." She didn't look at him as she slid past and out the front door of the station.

Regret twisted his insides. Maybe he was the one who needed to change. Maybe the events that had chiseled a canyon between them all those years ago were as much his fault as hers. But he couldn't rule out the fact that he'd never been able to apprehend the man who'd kidnapped her. He'd left no trail, only a damaged young woman with a knife wound in her chest a fraction away from her heart and a cold case that still gave him the creeps every time he opened the file box.

Now her father was dead. Murdered. But this time, he planned to find the culprit, no matter the risk. He couldn't let her down again.

RORY FOUND the silence inside the moving vehicle calming. Her thoughts were a tangle of partial information and the fear that the proverbial other shoe would drop. Was there more that Logan wasn't telling her about her father's death?

Still, as she eyed the darkness outside, she couldn't help but feel safer with him next to her.

Why her father had stayed in the area, she didn't know. Maybe it was his love for the mountain. Maybe it was the mystery surrounding the peak, which rose to eight-thousand feet from the valley floor. It wasn't a tall mountain, but it held a mystique most seemed unable to resist. For her it held memories too terrifying to comprehend.

"Would you like me to pick you up in the morning?" Logan asked.

The sound of his deep voice forced her out of her

thoughts. "I've got my car. I'll drive into town. You won't have to haul me home that way."

"I don't mind."

Why was he being so accommodating? Why, when she could feel the tension of unsaid words twisting him into knots.

He slowed the Blazer and pulled into the steep driveway for the quarter-mile descent. She tried to relax as he made the hairpin turns with precision. She swallowed the lump in her throat when the last corner came into view and he pulled into the driveway.

It was pitch black outside. She'd neglected to leave on the porch light.

He must have picked up on her apprehension because he killed the engine and left on the headlights. "I'll walk you in. Make sure you're settled."

Glancing in his direction, she saw the tension in his posture. "Thanks. I'd forgotten how off-the-beaten-path this place is."

Rory opened the door, climbed out and met him in front of the Blazer. "Geez, I hate nighttime here."

"You could always find a hotel in Cliff Side. Jenny Preston opened a little bed-and-breakfast in town, she'd probably love to see you again, and I wouldn't be worrying about you out here all alone."

"Is that a confession?"

"It's whatever you want it to be." He took her by the shoulders. "Just say the word."

She stared into his eyes, bright in the glare of the headlights. Her pulse jumped and she glanced at his lips. It was a fatal error, but she couldn't stop herself as she drew her arms up and around his neck.

He tensed and she felt his moment of hesitation just before his head came down.

Closing her eyes she anticipated the kiss before he crushed her to him, pushing the air from her lungs.

He kissed her. Softly at first, but then with a hunger she mirrored as she clung to him, drawing a moan from deep in his throat.

As quick as the passion had ensnared them both, it lifted, leaving her winded and confused.

Without a word she strode across the deck, pulled the house key from her jeans pocket and opened the screen door. Fiddling to get the key in, she heard him let out a breath, but didn't turn around.

He still had an effect on her. He still heated her blood to white-hot. He was dangerous and she'd do well to remember that in the days to come. Days she would need to spend close to him.

"Damn key."

"Here. Let me." He moved in next to her and took the key from her hand. Moving to the side, he let the full glow of the headlights shine on the lock.

"It's been jimmied. Did your dad lock himself out and have to pick his way in?"

"I don't know. It worked when I got here."

"The metal around the keyhole is flared. This lock's been tampered with."

Fear crept into her, its ripple effect moving

through her body and sending gooseflesh up on her arms. She swallowed hard. "Maybe we should try the back door. It takes the same key."

"Maybe you should get in the rig and lock the doors until I give you an all clear."

She wanted to argue, stand her ground and protest, but she peered into the darkness and decided his request made perfect sense.

Without a word she walked to the Blazer and climbed in.

Logan didn't move until he heard the locks engage. Unholstering his pistol, he moved away from the beams of the headlights and sucked up against the side of the cabin. He made his way around toward the back, listening for anything that might indicate there was someone inside.

The hair at his nape bristled as he stepped onto the concrete patio at the rear of the house.

Leaning around the rough-hewn beam at the corner of the cabin, he scanned the interior of the house where the headlights shone through the kitchen window.

Nothing. No movement. Only shadows.

Relief pulsed inside him as he stepped up to the door, which divided a pair of plate-glass windows. He slipped his gun back into its holster. Feeling the knob, he pushed the key into the lock.

The lock clicked. He turned the knob and opened the door. Reaching around the doorjamb, he felt for the light switch.

In one flick, the lights came on.

He stepped inside. Caution jumbled his nerves as he stared at the chaos.

The place had been ransacked. Torn apart piece by piece. That explained the jimmied front door.

An instant of relief spread through him. At least Rory hadn't been home. At least he didn't have to come here and find her, huddled, terrified…or worse.

He smoothed his hand over his head and swallowed the string of cuss words on the tip of his tongue.

Someone had been looking for something in the doctor's house.

But what?

Chapter Two

"Oh, no!"

Logan wheeled at the sound of Rory's voice from the doorway.

Her skin was ashen, her lips thinned in a hard line. But it was the terror in her eyes that undid his insides.

He'd seen that look before, high on Reaper's Point the day she was rescued from the near-fatal grasp of a killer. A killer he'd been unable to catch, much less identify. The bastard who stomped through his nightmares on a regular basis.

He moved toward her, bent on protecting her. But she sidestepped him and bolted down the short hallway leading to the bedrooms.

He was right behind her as she entered what, judging by the masculine furnishings, appeared to be her father's bedroom.

Rory dropped to the floor next to the bed and yanked up the bed skirt. "Thank God. They didn't find the safe."

"Pretty ingenious." Logan knelt next to her, staring at the long and narrow steel safe fitted neatly into the thick side-rail of the massive log bed.

"My dad was careful. He always protected what belonged to him."

Standing up, he pulled her to her feet. "I'm going to call Deputy Sparks. Have him come out and go over the whole place. Maybe the subject left a print. Can you check for missing items?"

"Yes." She pulled her hand out of his. Her cheeks flared red.

"Just remember. Look, don't touch."

"I've got it." She walked out of the bedroom and across the hall into her room. With a knuckle, she flipped on the light.

From the doorway, he watched her move around the room.

The dresser drawers had been pulled out and dumped. The closet doors stood wide-open. Mounds of clothing were heaped on the floor, where they'd been torn from hangers. The top shelf looked like it had been cleared by a twister.

"Whoever did this was packing some serious rage," she said.

Her comment echoed inside his head and raised his hackles. "You can't stay here tonight."

She turned on him, defiance in her green eyes, but as quickly as it'd come, it vanished. "I know."

"I've got a spare room at the condo."

Rory stared at Logan, sure the invitation had

come from his lips, but unable to stop the panic wiggling up her spine. She swallowed, considering the offer. Considering the risk.

"You said Jenny opened a B&B. I could go there—at least, until this place has been gone over."

"Let's give her a call." He chose that moment to smile. She didn't know why, but a measure of her fear evaporated.

She followed him out of the bedroom and into the living room where he picked up the phone and punched in a number. Studying him, she saw his shoulders stiffen.

"Jenny? Any chance you have a vacancy?"

He eyed her where she stood, but she knew what the answer was before he said his thanks and hung up the phone. "No luck. It's Friday and the place is full for the weekend. She'll have something available on Monday."

Processing the information set her nerves on edge. The nearest large motel was twenty-five miles away in Cliff Side. She was needed here.

"The condo it is."

His dark brown eyes took on a barely veiled twinkle. Her heart pounded in her chest. She swallowed. "You better call your deputy. It's getting late."

Walking into the kitchen she pulled a glass out of the cupboard and filled it at the sink. Over her shoulder, she heard him dial the phone, hang up and dial again, finally making contact with someone.

The glare of the headlights still shone through the kitchen window, creating eerie shadows in the trees surrounding the driveway.

A flash of movement caught her attention. She blinked. It was probably nothing but brush being stirred by the early fall wind.

Focusing until her vision blurred, she stared at the spot.

Like an apparition from a horror film, a human form took shape for an instant.

Before she could cap the scream rumbling up her throat, he stepped back into the shadows and vanished along with the last of her courage.

Logan was next to her in an second. "What?!"

"I saw someone. I saw a man step out of the shadows near the back of the Blazer." A shiver racked her body.

"I'll check it out."

"Please don't go out there," she begged, her voice cracking as she studied him. Six years of fear suddenly came crashing down. She wanted to run. Wanted to escape. Someplace where her control of her life wouldn't melt like chocolate on a hot day.

Logan wrapped his arms around her.

Burying her face against his chest, she breathed in a moment of peace before she pulled back. Snagged by doubt. He'd been unable to protect her six years ago. How could she expect him to do it now?

Dabbing her eyes, she tried to relax, but couldn't. "Shouldn't you wait for backup?"

"If I wait, he'll be long gone. Use the .38 on your hip if you need to. I'm going to check it out."

She could only nod, as fear, hard and cold, tensed her body. Her throat tightened.

"You can do this," Logan said, touching her cheek. "Just sit tight."

Looking into his eyes she found the reassurance she needed. She settled onto a stool at the counter and watched him unholster his gun before slipping out the front door.

She caught a glimpse of him through the kitchen window as he circled the Blazer and melded into the shadows where the man had vanished.

The seconds turned to minutes. She worked her thumb against the cold steel of the .38 hanging from her side. If only she'd had a weapon that day and been able to use it. If only… Maybe then she could have gotten away. She'd relived the scenario over and over in her mind these past six years, but she could never change the end.

Lost in myriad thought, she hardly noticed Logan duck into the headlights and slip in the door.

"You were right. There was someone out there. I tracked him to the trail just below the cabin, but he veered off somewhere before the aspen grove and I lost his trail."

"That path goes straight up the mountain on the

other side of the creek. Do you think it was him... the guy who tore this place apart?"

"That would be my guess. There's no one for miles around here. He could be holed up somewhere at the base of the mountain, or on the mountain itself."

Rory sucked in a breath. Concern worked her nerves into knots.

"Are you okay?" He slid his hand along her forearm, sending tiny shots of electricity through her body. "I will be. As soon as we get out of here."

"Hang on. Once Deputy Taylor arrives we'll get some pictures and dust for prints."

She nodded, feeling some of the tension leave her body. "I thought Sparks was coming?"

"He's off duty. I couldn't get an answer at his place."

Satisfied, she relaxed.

"What does your dad keep in the bed safe?"

"Papers, his will, tax records. A coin collection. Pretty ordinary stuff, not much value."

"Have you opened it yet?"

"No."

"Open it now. Make sure nothing inside has been disturbed or stolen. Let's rule out a simple burglary."

She stepped away from him, moved down the hall and into the bedroom. She'd hoped to open the safe later. There were personal mementos inside and she wasn't sure she was ready to sort through them just yet.

"It didn't look disturbed."

"We want to be sure. Keep your fingers on the ridging of the dial and use your palm on the tip of the handle. We don't want to destroy any possible fingerprints."

"I understand."

Logan pulled up the bed skirt and tucked it in between the mattress and box spring.

Rory knelt and turned the combination dial.

An ache squeezed inside his chest as he studied the top of her head. A head covered with the most luscious hair he'd ever had the pleasure of touching. She was as beautiful now as she'd been the day she ran away, leaving him with a hole in his heart and a cold case box on his desk. He didn't blame her. Hell, he blamed himself for what happened to her.

He heard the click of the safe lock, watched her force the lever up with her palm and shove backward.

The odor hit him like a freight train.

Decomposition.

"Dammit." He reached for her, bringing her to her feet as he stared into the safe.

"It's a femur," she whispered.

He held her close and took a step back, but she pulled away and moved to within inches of the safe and its contents.

"Adolescent, judging by the length. Why would my dad have something like this? Unless…" She turned to stare up at him. "He found it on the mountain and wanted to keep it safe."

"Along with the skull?" Foreboding hung in the air, making it hard for him to fill his lungs with anything but dread. Were they dealing with one body, or two? What the hell had Dr. Matson stumbled upon?

"I can analyze this femur. There will be surviving DNA in the marrow, if it isn't too deteriorated."

"Judging from the smell, I'd say something survived." He wasn't prepared for the knowing grin she flashed him or the instant zap of satisfaction that smoothed his muscles.

The rumble of an engine coming down the drive snapped him out of thought. "Taylor's here. We should be clear of the scene before midnight."

"Great." She stood up. "I'll go over my room, but I'd bet this is what the guy was after."

Caution festered inside of him. "If your dad uncovered a murder victim or a body dump, the assailant might be more than willing to kill again to cover it up."

"Yeah. So let's hope I can put an identity on that skull. The sooner we get a face out there the sooner we can discover who she was, where she came from and who might have wanted her dead."

He liked the way her mind worked. Always had, but now she was different somehow, sharper, more refined. Her job at the L.A. crime lab had turned her into an investigator, so why didn't he feel good about it? Why was there a tentacle of worry winding through him and tightening as the seconds ticked by?

Her abductor had never been caught. Was it possible he was still out there, roaming the trails and woods of Reaper's Point?

What if Rory was the only one who'd gotten away?

Were there others?

A chill bit into him as he left the room, anxious to document the scene and get her home where he could keep her safe.

RORY STARED at the four-poster bed and envisioned herself falling into it. The only part of the vision that disturbed her was the fact that Logan was with her.

She closed the door and leaned against it. She'd gotten him out of her system, hadn't she? Of course it had been a forced cleansing, brought on by a madman's assault. Just the thought of being touched ever again had been too much to get over and so she'd run like a frightened child. Run like her life depended on it.

She pushed away from the door, intent on a good night's sleep. Morning would come much too soon and the mountain beckoned, surrounded in a mystery as thick as the clouds that sometimes covered its summit.

Slipping out of her jeans and T-shirt, she donned her nightie and turned on the bedside lamp, before shutting off the light switch. Her body craved sleep, but her mind was on fire with questions. Questions that could only be answered by a trek up Reaper's Point and a rendezvous with her past.

A rap at the door startled her. "Yeah?"

"Can I come in?"

A moment of indecision glided through her brain as she weighed the consequences of letting a man like Logan in. "Just a minute."

Pulling back the covers, she slid in between the sheets and pulled the blankets up to her neck. "Okay."

The door opened.

He stood in the frame, shirtless. "I trust this will do until you can move into the B&B."

"Yeah. It's perfect." She knew what was perfect. Him standing at the threshold of her room. When had she become a prude? When had she given up on ever feeling anything for the opposite sex?

Five years, two hundred and thirty-eight days, four hours and ten minutes ago.

She closed her eyes for a moment to clear her head. "It's been a horrific day, Logan. Thanks for being there for me."

"You're welcome." He stepped closer.

Caution pushed through her, raising her defenses. "Tomorrow is going to come too early."

Still he moved toward her.

"I'm really tired tonight."

"I bet." He stopped at the foot of the bed.

Relief spread over her.

"Just say it, Rory. Tell me what went wrong between us?"

She swallowed, trying to find words that would

push him away. Drive him from her life again, but she had lost them. Where was the blame she'd used to justify running away from her fear?

"I can't. I don't know."

He came around the bed and sat down on the edge. "You know I did everything I could."

"Everything but catch the bastard."

He looked down, the muscle along his jaw tightened. "He was mist. I climbed that damn mountain every day until the first snow, looking for him. There were signs that someone had camped, but everything had been cleaned meticulously. If he was still up there, he was invisible. But I never stopped trying to find him. To bring him to justice for what he did to you. To us."

Her throat closed. Her eyes burned with unshed tears as she stared at him. At the man she'd loved once upon a time…before a vicious killer had stripped her life away and left her for dead.

The physical scars had healed, but it was the ones on the inside that refused to respond to treatment of any kind.

"It wasn't enough. I haven't felt safe since that day."

"I'm sorry." His head dropped.

She fought the need to touch him. To brush away the pain that radiated from him with an energy that muddied her resolve.

"I need to sleep."

"Me, too." He stood up and strode to the door,

giving her one more glance before he left the room, closing the door behind him.

She couldn't hold back the tears. What was this place doing to her? Hadn't she unpacked this baggage years ago? She certainly had the therapy bills to prove it.

Wiping her eyes, she flopped down on the pillow and tried to relax, tried to shut out the images that had escaped the prison she'd closed them in.

Her attacker was still out there. And, try as she might, that was something she could never escape.

Chapter Three

"Good morning, sunshine."

Rory managed a smile even though her eyes felt like they'd been rolled in sand and her brain entombed in the castle.

"Still a morning person, I see."

"Yeah." He pulled a mug from the cupboard above the coffeemaker and poured her a cup as she slid onto a stool at the bar.

She watched him put three teaspoons of sugar and a splash of cream into the cup and give it a quick stir. He remembered just how she liked it. An odd sensation of longing zipped through her as he sat the cup in front of her.

"Drink up. We'll have some breakfast in town and go to the station. Deputy Sparks is going to make the trip up the mountain with us. He shot all the pictures at the scene."

She put the cup to her lips and sucked in a gulp of the rich java. She'd always loved his coffee. She hadn't tasted anything that even came close for a long time now.

"Good." She put her cup down. "I want to get that femur packaged and out to my lab. Maybe we'll get lucky and get something off of it."

He leaned casually against the counter. His white T-shirt pulled taut over his hard chest. Every bulge and bump accentuated in vivid detail.

Her mouth went dry. She tried not to stare, but she'd have to be blind not to realize how gorgeous he was.

"Your old climbing gear is here."

"I'm not going to climb."

He stared at her. His silence doing more to unnerve her than the actual fear she felt.

"Ever." She added, watching him gaze at her intently through knowing brown eyes, as if doing so would somehow open up her secrets for his scrutiny.

"I'm sorry. Of course you won't ever climb again, but the equipment is here if you change your mind."

"I won't." She took another drink from her mug, studying him over the rim. What the hell was he thinking, expecting her to climb? That was a part of her life that was gone, along with the ties she'd had with him and Reaper's Point.

"I'll hop in the shower and get dressed." She finished the last of her coffee and sat the cup in the sink, aware of how close they stood to one another and just how far apart they really were.

"I'm glad you came back, Rory."

"I had to. For my dad." She swallowed. It was difficult to think of her life without her father. The years since her abduction and subsequent departure had altered their relationship, but at least he'd finally consented to coming down from his cabin for regular visits with her in L.A. There they'd sightsee and explore the city, just as they had the mountain.

"He was doing great." Logan let out a long sigh. "Still knew the mountain better than anyone around here."

"I know. And that may have gotten him killed."

He turned to stare out the kitchen window at Reaper's Point.

She turned with him. Drawn by the majestic beauty of the mountain, with its deep ravines and granite faces sweeping up to a sharp peak. Deadly, in a beautiful sort of way.

"You're right. But why would your father hide the femur and skull? Protect them, instead of bringing them into the sheriff's office along with a map of the location where he found them?"

"I don't know. What else did you find in his backpack?"

"The remains of a half-eaten lunch, a compass and some clothing."

Curiosity edged her nerves. "No climbing gear, extra carabiners, hooks…anything?"

"No. Looked like a day pack to me."

"Last month, he told me he had decided to quit climbing. His knees were bothering him. It would require a miracle to heal that fast."

"Who's his doctor?"

"Hatley over in Cliff Side."

"Maybe we better call him. Find out how bad your dad's knees were. It would prove that he didn't go up there to climb and that the gear we found on him would have had to have been provided by the killer."

Tension knotted the muscles between her shoulder blades. "Great. The plot thickens." She turned and left the kitchen.

Logan stared after her, memorizing the sway of her hips. There was a time when he would have chased her back to the bedroom. But that time had ended—abruptly.

He turned and put his mug in the sink next to hers. Today would try her. Unmask the terror he knew still raged beneath the surface. If there were another way, he'd like to find it, but his gut told him otherwise. Dr. Matson had been murdered on Reaper's Point and he needed Rory's help and insight to get at the truth.

"WHAT IS THAT?" Rory asked.

Logan followed her line of sight, letting his gaze settle on the white cardboard box sitting on his desk. It was marked A. Matson, but it was the words underneath her name that made his heart squeeze. Cold Case.

"I'm planning to go through it again since you're in town."

She turned away from him and headed for the break room. He watched her leave. Once again he'd played cop instead of tactful man. It was a mistake, he realized, but not before he heard the door slam shut.

"Problem?" Deputy Sparks entered the front door and paused.

"Yeah. One that should have been solved years ago."

"Her cold case?"

"I'd have given anything to have caught the bastard, but he was too slick. I know I was on top of him a couple of times, but he always managed to be a step ahead."

"Reaper's Point covers twenty thousand square miles. A man could disappear up there and never be seen again."

"I know." Regret pounded deep in his chest. "Did you find any footprints you could cast along the trail out at Matson's place this morning?"

"I found a shoe print next to the edge of the driveway. I casted it, but the path into the woods was clear."

"He didn't leave anything inside," Logan said.

"Probably wore gloves."

Concern laced his nerves. They weren't dealing with an amateur. "You have that casting?"

"In evidence. It should be good and dry by

now." Sparks put down the clipboard he'd signed in on and headed for the evidence room at the rear of the station.

Logan snagged the cold case box off his desk and followed. If it made Rory uncomfortable, then he'd accommodate her, go over the case somewhere out of sight.

He sat the box down on the counter and turned to where Sparks lifted the plaster cast of the shoe print out of a sealed container.

"It's the ball of the right foot judging by the curve of the outer edge."

Logan stared at the casting, a knot forming in his gut. He'd know that brand of shoe tread anywhere. He'd studied it at least a hundred times. It hadn't been manufactured for more than two years.

Like a man in a trance he turned to the evidence box on the counter and pulled off the lid. He'd memorized everything inside, but he had to be sure. Reaching in he lifted out the shoe tread casting, carefully wrapped and protected against damage.

"No way!" Sparks's comment only worked to set his belief in stone.

Peeling back the protective plastic cover he turned and put the casting down on the counter next to the casting from outside the Matson's cabin.

Fear and determination mingled in his blood, as he visually compared them. He ground his teeth together. "They match."

Sparks let out a long, low whistle. "I don't be-lieve it. He's back."

"Who's back?" Rory felt like she'd just walked in on a couple of boys spying through a hole in the shower stall of the girls' locker room. Concern zipped through her as she focused on Logan's face.

His jaw was set. His dark brown eyes had taken on the gleam of some secret excitement she wanted to be a part of, but her gaze drifted to the open lid of her cold case box, only to settle on the castings lined up next to one another on the counter.

She tried to breathe normally but couldn't. There wasn't any air in the room. Her knees buckled but Logan was there to catch her.

He was back?

The bastard who'd almost killed her six years ago was here in Reaper's Point? The matching shoe print proved he'd been outside the cabin last night. Watching. Waiting.

Terror coursed through her. It took everything she had not to run. Again.

"I'm sorry, Rory," Logan said, pulling her closer.

The soothing tone of his voice in her ear sent shivers through her. She leaned into him. He'd done the same for her before she'd been airlifted from the mountain, but she'd pulled away.

Not this time. She needed him. Needed his pro-tection.

"I'll get him this time. I won't let him escape. I promise."

She pushed back, staring up into his face. Palpable determination oozed from him, showing in the set of his jaw. The steely hardness in his gaze.

"We'll get him…together."

"Are you sure about this?" Logan asked, his features softening.

"As sure as I've ever been."

He smiled at her and her fear subsided. The madman she'd been running from was right here in Reaper's Point. Again. She'd come full circle, but she was stronger and smarter this time.

"Do you suppose my father stumbled onto his camp up there?"

"More likely a body dump."

Uneasiness slid through her veins, warring with her fight or flight response. He'd killed. She wasn't his only victim, but maybe the only one who'd escaped.

"It's the only thing that makes sense, Rory. Somewhere on Reaper's Point he stumbled on a body. Several, for all we know. He brought the femur down and hid it, maybe he feared for his life."

"Yeah. He's dead. I'd say his fear was realized."

"Maybe the skull was at the same site or maybe he discovered it somewhere else. The only way to know is to get up on the mountain. Try to retrace his steps."

A chill skittered through her body that not even the fire in Logan's eyes could melt.

Deputy Sparks was already pulling on a pair

of gloves so he wouldn't damage any evidence that might be on the backpack. "Your dad was wearing it when we found him. There was nothing to suggest it had been opened or tampered with. Everything was stacked carefully inside," the deputy said.

"He was a neat freak." She managed a smile, remembering how particular he'd been about everything.

She watched Sparks undo the latch and open the top of the pack, before carefully removing everything from inside and laying it out on the table.

Pulling a pair of gloves out of the dispenser box, she slipped them on and picked up a piece of paper folded in quarters. She opened it, studying the series of squiggly lines that all seemed to intersect in the middle of the page.

She turned it slowly, hoping for a hint of recognition. It could be a map. What if her father had used it to find the bones again? It was crude, but it could represent the drainages from the mountaintop.

"Do you have a topographical map of Reaper's Point?"

"In my office, on the wall."

They strode into Logan's office.

Excitement churned her stomach and tightened her nerves. "If he used the lines to indicate drainage points…" With her finger she moved in a counterclockwise direction, counting every drainage that carried runoff away from Reaper's Point when the snow melted.

"Seven." Next she counted the number of lines on the sheet of paper her father had scribbled. Seven. "If it's a map, there aren't any points of reference. Without those, it's just a piece of paper."

She stepped back from the map. Frustration hissed in her veins. "We could search every ravine."

"That's treacherous country. No one goes in there," Sparks said.

"Well, someone did." Rory glanced at Logan. "What better place to hide than a virtual no-man's-land. You could survive undetected for months."

Logan watched from the end of the table, worry kneading his muscles into knots. The image of Rory when they'd found her nude and almost lifeless body after the abduction was still burned into his brain in detail.

"You're not going up there, Aurora."

She glared at him, but he couldn't mistake the brief look of relief in her eyes. He couldn't let her be hurt again and if that meant she stayed off of Reaper's Point until hell froze over, then so be it. Everything had changed for him the moment he'd made the casting match.

"Sparks and I can handle it. He'll get you the pictures of the scene. Maybe you can find something we missed. Then we'll head up the mountain."

"You won't get an argument from me. Besides,

my kit should be here sometime this morning. I'd like to get started on the skull."

"Overnight deliveries usually show up around ten." Logan straightened.

"Great, you have time to run me out to my dad's place. I need to grab the rest of my stuff. I'm not going to stay there alone."

"Stay at my place for as long as you like."

She gazed at him, gratitude in her eyes. His insides turned to putty.

"If I can cast the skull today, you can ship it out tomorrow along with the femur for DNA testing. We can establish if we're looking at a single individual or multiple victims."

He looked away, only long enough to regain his equilibrium. She'd always rocked his world, but he was surprised by how fast it had happened this time. How quickly the dying embers had flashed, hot and viable.

"Sparks can package them as soon as you're finished. Let's head up to the cabin."

He watched her hand the useless map to the deputy and peel off the latex gloves. "There's a chance we're looking at a single individual. There could have been animal activity around the remains. Things get dragged off and dispersed."

"Let's hope." He didn't want to probe too deeply into the idea that there were more than one set of remains on the mountain, at least, not with her. And with any luck they'd find out the bones belonged to a missing hiker who'd taken a wrong turn and a wrong step into a ravine. But a forensic examination would be able to determine cause of death.

"Sparks. Pull everything we have on missing persons known to have been in or coming to this area. If we can get a list of names and their DNA profiles out of the missing persons database, we'll be a step ahead of the game."

"I'll get on it." Sparks left the office.

"When did you start using the system?"

"After your abduction. It made sense to get a profile on record. We started having families bring in the missing person's hairbrush, toothbrush— anything we could pull a sample from. Reaper's Point doesn't give up its dead very easily. At least, when it does, we now have a way to let the next of kin know we've found them."

"Makes sense." She moved around the desk. "Let's get going. I'm anxious to get back here and make a casting of the skull for the reconstruction."

"Sure." He followed her out of the evidence room, through the office and out the front door.

The day was sunny and crisp. The tourist season was winding down. Before long the tiny town would empty of summer people and the snow would come.

"This place has grown since I left."

He opened the passenger-side door of the Blazer for her. "Seems to get worse every year." He closed the door, made his way around to the drivers side and climbed in.

"It can't be too bad for the local economy."

"It's great for the economy, just not for the peace-loving locals who find it all too much."

"My dad is—was, one of those."

"What I said back there about your dad never giving up, I meant it. He roamed the mountain every summer. He claimed he was just studying the flora and the conifers, but I didn't buy a word of it. He was looking for the man who took you."

"Thanks for that." She turned and stared out the window.

Logan fired the engine and backed out of the parking space. He'd been fond of Dr. Matson. He had a brilliant mind and a beautiful daughter, both huge draws.

He turned out onto the main north-south highway and cruised through town before beginning the ascent up the narrow road that snaked partway up the mountain, ending at a huge parking lot called Base-Camp. It was the starting point for most people's treks up the mountain. The Matson cabin was several miles below Base-Camp, situated at the bottom of a steep draw.

The police radio crackled to life with a squelch.

"Sheriff Brewer. Belle County dispatch. What's your twenty?"

The hiss of radio traffic set Rory's nerves on edge. Logan casually pulled the handset from its holder and up to his mouth. "Copy that, Belle County dispatch. I'm northbound on twenty-six."

"I have a report of an unknown disturbance in the Base-Camp parking lot."

"Copy, dispatch. Any more details?"

"Negative. The 9-1-1 call came in on a cell phone. Broken traffic."

"Copy. I'm en route. Zero-five-eight-seven-three clear." Logan clipped the radio microphone back into its holder. "Hang on, we're going lights and siren."

Rory felt her stomach drop as he accelerated up the curvy road. She wanted to close her eyes, but doing so would only serve in making her more tense. "Can you drop me off?"

"Sorry. It'll have to wait until after the call. It's probably routine. Lost or stolen climbing gear. A missing car stereo."

She settled into the seat, watching the terrain flash by the window, unable to relax. They were headed to the spot she'd been airlifted from, barely alive.

The dark memories taunted her. Pulling her back into the shadows. She'd been unable to describe her abductor or the location where he'd taken her. With such limited information, the case had gone cold in a heartbeat.

Logan braked for an instant before accelerating around the last curve and pulling into the lot.

Several cars were parked at the far end.

A group of climbers waved frantically when they spotted the Blazer.

"Sit tight. I'll see what the problem is and have you home before lunch." He pulled forward and stopped the rig. Climbing out, he focused on the couple coming toward him at a jog.

Striding forward, he met them halfway. "What's the problem?"

"Our hiking partner, Sid—" out of breath, the female hiker clad in red neoprene pointed back at the crowd "—saw something beside the trail."

Logan's nerves tensed. "What did he see?"

"I can't be sure, he's torn up about it...but, I swear, I heard him say it was a woman's...body."

An instant of fear furrowed his nerves, then eroded to caution.

"I need to talk to him." Logan strode toward the handful of climbers crowded around a young man in his early twenties.

They parted as he approached, only to find the witness bent over at the waist, puking his guts out.

"Are you Sid?"

Someone handed the witness a towel and he wiped his face. "Yeah."

"Want to tell me what you saw up there?" Logan gestured to the mountain.

"A body." Sid heaved again, but there was nothing left to expel.

"Are you sure? Can you take me to the place where you believe you saw it?"

"Yes." He straightened, taking a couple of wobbly steps. "I took off, first, up the Clear Creek trailhead. I made it to the first wide bend. I stopped for a water break. That's when I looked over the edge into the draw, and...there she was." He leaned forward again.

Logan looked over his head at the Blazer. "Take it easy for a minute. I'm going to call for backup."

Sid could only nod, he was too busy turning his stomach inside out for anything else.

Logan hurried to the rig to call in the team and retrieve his handheld radio.

"Is everything okay?" Rory asked.

He stared at her for a moment. Could he tell her? Could he express the dread that had invaded his mind and body only moments ago?

"No. A hiker appears to have seen a body in the ravine near Clear Creek. I'm going to call in backup and head up there. Want to come?"

For an instant fear glowed in her eyes like a distant fire, but it went out. He watched her unbuckle her seat belt and reach for the door handle.

"I'd rather go than stay here in the lot."

His throat tightened with realization. This was where he'd taken her in his arms and promised to bring in the madman who'd tried to kill her. But he'd failed. Miserably.

"It's a hike."

"I can hack it, Brewer. I've been kickboxing at the gym—five days a week for the past three years."

"Okay." He snagged his backpack off the rear seat, and she put it on while he talked to the dispatcher over the two-way radio.

She was right there next to him as he helped a sickly looking Sid stand up. Then they all trudged up the steep trail at the base of the mountain.

He knew they were close when Sid started to slow down. He could see the hesitation in his steps. Feel the beginnings of his fear as it worked to change reasonable thought into a jumble of terror. "She's up here, on the right."

"You don't have to go any farther. You can stop if you like."

Sid plopped down on a rock, holding his stomach. "Thank God."

He stared at Rory, willing her to take a seat next to Sid, whose complexion matched the pine needles on the trees, but she wasn't going to sit this one out. There was determination in her eyes as she returned his gaze.

Without a word he continued along the trail, careful of the loose rocks along the edge. Careful to look for signs of a crime.

Then he spotted a nude female body, fifty feet down, laying in a thick patch of brush. She looked like a rag doll who'd been tossed away.

His stomach squeezed. He pulled air into his lungs, trying to get his emotions under control.

They were going to need Search and Rescue to bring her up out of the draw.

A gasp reminded him he wasn't alone at this horrific scene. He turned to look at Rory.

The color was gone from her face, her lips pulled in a grim line.

"It's him," she whispered in a voice so soft he had to lean closer.

"What?"

"Her hands are tied in front of her and she's blindfolded."

He knew exactly what she was talking about. He'd looked down at her in a ravine six years ago and the image was still burned into his brain.

"He restrained me just like that. It's his M.O."

Rage and caution mixed in his blood as he pulled her into his arms and felt her shudder.

The madman was back.

Chapter Four

Rory's head throbbed. Her stomach revolting as she fought the sick sensation rolling around inside of her. In a wash of emotion, she relived that horrible day, down to the last horrific act that had been inflicted on her.

A knife blade in the chest.

Drawing strength from Logan, she pulled back and looked up into his face. "We have to see if she's alive."

"What are the odds?"

She glanced back down into the ravine, tension knotting her muscles. "I survived, didn't I? There's always a chance."

Logan pulled the pack off his back and opened the flap, taking out his climbing rope and a seat harness.

Instinctively, she helped him put on the gear. It was amazing how little she'd forgotten, even though she'd tried.

Logan tied off to a strapping pine tree and looped his rope through a figure-eight descender. He clipped it onto the carabiner he'd snapped onto the front of his harness. It was a simple method, but effective. He pulled his backpack on and straightened.

Tension built along Rory's nerves. She watched him toss the coiled rope over the edge of the trail ledge, then don his helmet.

"Be careful."

"I always am. Search and Rescue should be here in half an hour."

"I'll be here."

He smiled at her, but she could see the dread in his eyes, knew the hopelessness of the situation had already eaten a hole in him.

Logan leaned back against the rope, testing its strength before feeding it through the descender attached to the front of his harness. He shuffled off the edge of the trail.

Rock gave way under his feet as he traversed well to the left of where the woman lay, careful not to send anything down on her and destroy evidence in the process.

He studied the terrain, looking for anything the killer may have left.

Twenty feet. He paused for a moment to get his bearings, glancing up at Rory, where she stood, watching him intently. He gave her a thumbs-up and proceeded to work his way the rest of the way down, pausing to tie off at fifty-five feet.

His heartbeat drummed in his ears as he surveyed the area around the body, before looking directly at her.

She wasn't moving.

He focused on her for signs of life.

Nothing.

Pressing through the brush, he studied the ground for prints, but it had been swept clean.

Whoever had dumped the body knew what they were doing. Dammit. It would only make solving the case that much harder. If he was able to solve it at all.

A knot formed in his stomach and turned to granite.

Moving closer, Logan spotted a single knife wound to the chest, straight into the heart, just like the one Rory had suffered. But the bastard had missed that time. Not so, this time. And there was something else strange. Seven deep cuts in succession across her forehead.

He glanced up and saw Rory step back from the edge of the trail.

The sound of voices caught his attention. He recognized the Search and Rescue boys as they lined up along the edge of the trail to assess the situation.

"Is she alive?" one shouted down to him.

Logan gave an overexaggerated head shake in the negative. Then pulled off his backpack. Opening it he took out his camera to document the scene before Search and Rescue did their job. What he'd hoped would be a rescue, would be a recovery.

Anger and determination coursed through him as he shot frame after frame of the victim. With each click of the lens his concern built, until he thought he'd explode. If he'd doubted for a second that Rory's abductor was back, that notion had now faded along with any qualms he had about keeping her safe. He could only hope this murder would produce some clues. Something they could go on.

RORY FOUGHT THE URGE to join Sid on the rock where he still sat. Her stomach hadn't stopped turning since she'd watched Logan confirm that the young woman in the ravine was dead.

"You must be Aurora Matson."

She turned to face the man who'd addressed her, shading her eyes against the sun.

"Rory, please. And you are?"

"Brady Morris, Search and Rescue. Your dad showed me your picture. In fact, more than once."

"How did you meet?"

"I consulted your father when we had a difficult rescue, or lost hikers. He really knew this mountain."

"Yes, he did."

"I'm sorry for your loss."

"Thanks."

Brady turned away from her and moved to where his coworkers prepared their equipment for the over-the-bank operation. He seemed like a nice guy. Her dad had had a lot of friends in Reaper's Point.

Rory swallowed and glanced back down into the ravine where Logan was putting his camera back into his pack. The sun glinted off his dark hair. Her mouth went dry. He'd found himself in the middle of a murder case. She didn't envy him. At least she was physically removed from the gruesome details of this scene.

She closed her eyes for an instant to still her jittery nerves. When she opened them again, Logan had donned his backpack and was making his way up out of the steep ravine, a few steps at a time, drawing his rope tight from the rear to keep the tension. Her guesstimate put the slope at a seventy-five degree angle. Not a place for an amateur, but Logan wasn't an amateur.

Admiration surged in her mind as she watched the precise calculation of his movements. It was like watching a ballet. Each move executed precisely, blending and connecting into a whole. Weight back, trust in the rope, keep the tension.

That had been the hardest thing for her to learn. Putting all her trust in a piece of rope. Leaning back and walking up a mountain.

Defying gravity.

She watched Logan pace himself, watched his arms flex and bulge as he climbed closer to the edge.

Ping.

The sound of the rope breaking whistled in her ears.

In slow motion, the end flicked high into the air like a whip.

Fear pounded in her mind as her stare locked on Logan.

He clawed with both hands, but there was nothing to grab on to.

A scream tore from her mouth as he flew backward, launched by the tension now released from the rope.

In one horrifying second, he went airborne, his guttural growl of disbelief resounding in her ears.

She closed her eyes when she heard the first thud. The second came close behind.

Staggering to the edge of the trail along with the Search and Rescue team, she dared to stare down into the draw, just as Logan tumbled one more time and came to a stop one-hundred feet below.

Helpless energy pulsed in her body as she beat back fear.

He wasn't moving.

Her throat closed, her heart rate skyrocketed. She teetered on the edge of the trail, caught between paralyzing fear and the primal need to act.

She had to get to him.

Now.

Glancing around she spotted a pile of climbing gear and raced for it. Picking up a harness, she had it on and was about to fasten it, when she felt a hand on her arm.

In a panic she looked up into Brady Morris' face.

"Hold on. We're ready, we're going down."

She tried to protest, but his grip on her arm tightened.

"Forget it, Matson. You're not qualified. Let us do our job."

She stared up into his face. His mouth was hardened in a tight smile, his eyes, slate-gray and hard as stone.

Rory swallowed and gave a nod.

Brady released her arm and stepped back. "Stay put. We'll get him out of there."

A shudder rippled through her as she sank down into a sitting position, too drained to move.

One by one, the team went over the bank. She watched the flex and pull of their ropes where they'd tied off to several mammoth tree trunks. Gradually, her gaze settled on what was left of Logan's rope. Her breath caught in her throat as she stood up and moved in for a closer look.

His tie-off knot had held. Grasping the rope she pulled it through her hand. The smooth feel of the nylon against her fingers was reassuring. It was in great condition. No wear. No frayed fibers.

Inch by inch, she pulled it up, feeling for anything that might explain why he was laying in the bottom of the ravine.

Five feet. Four. Three. The end of the rope crested

the lip of the trail. She pulled it up, studying the break.

Realization pounded inside of her as she rubbed her fingers against the breaking point.

A clean cut ringed the nylon rope, an eighth-of-an-inch deep. The core was frayed and stretched.

His rope had been deliberately compromised. There was no way it could do its job if Logan put weight on it for a prolonged period of time.

Someone wanted to hurt him—or worse.

"He's alive!"

The sound of a rescuer's voice echoed from deep in the gully.

Rory dropped the rope and hurried to the edge. She focused on Logan, surrounded by rescue workers. He was sitting up. A good sign, she guessed, but he was far from being up out of the draw.

He stood up with help, but she watched him wobble and go down. Her heart sagged. There were any number of internal injuries he could be suffering from.

A rescue worker gave a shout and the litter was tied to a rope at the top and bottom.

She watched it slide down the steep grade.

The minutes passed like hours. Finally, she saw Logan climb into the litter. The team packaged him, and the arduous task of bringing him up the slope began.

She didn't breathe properly until he was hoisted up onto the trail.

She moved close to him, staring at the splint on his lower leg. "Is it broken?"

"Yeah. Thank God that's all that's wrong."

She swallowed. Fighting the need to touch him. To make sure he was all right under his macho exterior, but she didn't get the chance. Brady Morris stepped in between them.

"We're going to transport him to the hospital in Cliff Side. His leg is broken. Do you want to ride along?"

Logan stared up at Rory and Brady Morris. An instant of caution zipped through him as he watched Morris touch her arm and saw her instinctively withdraw.

A wave of guilt washed over him. Even casual contact bothered her. He couldn't blame her after what she gone through on this mountain and now there was another victim. It had to be at the front of her mind.

"Yes. I want to come along." She stared down at him, worry in her eyes.

"I'm going to live, Rory. It's nothing a cast and eight weeks won't take care of." His observation didn't relax the crease between her eyebrows.

"Sheriff?"

Logan tried to raise his head at the sound of Deputy Sparks's voice, but the damn C-collar around his neck held him immobile. "Take this off. I didn't break my neck on the way down."

"Sorry, Sheriff. You know the drill," Morris said.

Logan could swear he saw Brady crack a smile just before he turned away.

"Sparks. I'm glad you're here. I took photos of the scene, but you need to check the camera. It tumbled down with me. You might need to shoot another roll if it's damaged."

"Okay. Anything else?"

"No. They're taking me to Cliff Side Memorial. I'll see you back at the station as soon as they cut me loose."

Brady was giving the orders. Four members of the team picked up the litter and started down the trail.

Rory lagged behind with Sparks for a minute. "Hey." She watched the team disappear around the bend. "Be sure you collect the end of Logan's rope from around that tree." She pointed out the exact one. "I'm sure it was cut to weaken it."

Surprise slipped over his features. "I'll collect it and the other end, too."

"Thanks."

"No problem."

"I'll see you this afternoon." She turned and started down the trail.

"Your kit arrived just before I left the station."

She paused. "Great. Thanks." She moved forward again, picking up her pace so she could catch up with the team.

Rory broke into a fast walk, aware of the chill on the breeze stirring the pines. There was a winter storm in the air. She could feel it even though the sun was shining and the sky was void of clouds. She rounded the bend in the trail, prepared to see Search and Rescue, but they weren't there.

They were making good time, she decided as she continued along the path, determined to catch up with them.

Uneasiness sliced through her as she ducked under a low branch and walked into the shadows created by a grove of tall pines.

Caution skittered over her nerves as she stopped short, staring into the surrounding woods.

Was she being watched? Or just being paranoid?

She scanned the brush for movement, panic taking hold. She swallowed and sucked in a deep breath to still the unreasonable fear inside of her.

The forest was alive. It always had been. She'd loved that about being on the mountain.

Rory closed her eyes, determined to make peace in the battle raging inside of her.

She listened to the breeze stir the leaves on the aspen trees next to the trail. A rustle that ebbed and waned with the wind. High in the tops of the pines, wind moved against their needles making them whisper in some secret timeless language she couldn't understand.

Pulling in a breath, she relaxed. The hardy smell of pitch hung in the air, released by the heat of the day.

To her left a branch snapped, breaking her peaceful recollection abruptly.

Her eyes flew open and she fought the urge to bolt. If she let her overactive imagination control her, she'd be in real trouble. Afraid of her own shadow and everyone else's. She had to get control of her fear. Somehow.

Moving forward, she broke into a jog and burst out on the other side of the trees. For an instant the sun blinded her.

In a flash, she collided with someone. She felt his hands squeeze her forearms.

Panic rocked her body.

"Geez, lady. Watch where you're going."

Rory sucked in a breath as her vision focused on the scruffy looking man holding her.

She wrenched out of his grasp and stepped back, making a mental note of his appearance.

He had a full beard, gray. A grungy ball cap pulled down around his ears. His hair dished out from under it.

He wasn't a hiker or a climber. They wouldn't be caught dead here without their designer ware.

"Sorry. Did you happen to see a rescue team up ahead?"

"Yeah, just around the next corner. If you hurry, you can catch them."

He moved past her and continued up the trail. She stared after him, an odd sensation in her gut. He seemed out of place here.

Turning, she jogged down the trail, determined to get off Reaper's Point while she could still think straight.

LOGAN DIDN'T RELAX until Rory climbed into the back of the ambulance and the doors closed behind her.

"Does it hurt much?" She eyed the air-splint the E.M.T.s had inflated on his lower left leg.

"Only when I breathe, but I'll live." He would live and feel better doing it as long as he could keep her close. Seeing the dead woman on the mountain had hammered worry so deep into his brain, he'd never get it out. Protecting her was going to be the only antidote.

"What happened up there?" She glanced at the E.M.T. who was taking Logan's vitals before they put the ambulance on the road.

"My rope snapped. It was the damnedest thing, I just inspected it last week." He watched her frown and fidget.

The E.M.T. sat back at the head of the gurney and spoke into his portable microphone. "We're clear."

The ambulance driver rolled out of the parking lot, headed for the hospital in Cliff Side.

Rory leaned in close to him.

His heart rate climbed. Tiny beads of sweat formed on his forehead. He had to get this damn C-collar off before he went nuts. He stared up at her, unable to turn his head from side to side.

"I took a look at your rope. Someone deliberately cut it, knowing it would break when you put weight on it."

Caution rolled through him as he gazed up at her. "I've got a hunch you're right. Let's talk about it in private, after they cast my leg."

"Okay." She sat back for the ride to the hospital.

He tried to relax, but his mind was spinning. Why had his rope been deliberately compromised?

Why would someone want him maimed or, worse, dead?

"YOU LUCKED OUT, Brewer." Rory took a permanent marker out of the pencil can on Logan's desk and pulled off the cap. "If your rope had failed farther up the trail, I might be signing a body cast."

She glanced at his face for a record of his reaction, but he was unreadable. They'd taken a look at the end of the rope under a microscope and everyone had agreed, the rope had been cut just enough that it would fail at some point if it were used and, since Logan had inspected it earlier, the time window was well established. The rope had been compromised within the last week.

Bending over the desk where he had his leg propped up, Rory wrote her name in big sprawling letters and capped the marker.

"Aren't you going to include a message?" He looked at her and smiled.

"Yeah. Don't go to Reaper's Point."

His smile faded and the air in the room thickened. "You can't run from it, Rory."

"Wanna bet?" She moved back to the chair in front of the desk and sat down, feeling her own disquiet mix with his. "It's really easy to stay off the mountain. If we don't go up, we can't be hurt."

If her words triggered a reaction inside of him, it didn't show on his face. He studied her, making her more uncomfortable as the moments passed.

"I'm sorry, Aurora. Sorry as hell I didn't catch him."

A shudder tumbled over her. She swallowed against the constriction in her throat. "You're going to get another chance. How many of us ever get that?"

He lifted his chin and she saw him clamp his teeth together. Did she see a hint of fear in his eyes? The Logan she knew was hardy, prepared and protective, but she had blamed him all those years ago for someone else's actions. Did he blame himself, too?

"I think it might be time to call in the FBI. I'm not sure this department can handle a case this size."

She relaxed into the chair. "You might be right, but let me cast the skull first and send the bones to the lab. If the FBI takes them, getting them back will be next to impossible and I want to know why my father thought it was important enough to have them in his possession."

He considered her for a moment and she saw his resolve soften. "Go your best. You can use Sparks to help if you need him."

"Thanks." She stood up, feeling a new burst of energy. She'd be in her element at the lab, on familiar ground. The thought gave her a moment's peace. Science was the only thing that had saved her mentally after the attack. Putting known facts together had allowed her to shield herself from the outside world, where chaos and uncertainty ruled. Unfortunately, she'd felt that chaos closing in that morning on Reaper's Point, but she didn't plan to ever let that bone-racking fear control her mind or her body again.

Deputy Sparks stepped into the doorway of the office, a smile on his face. "It's all set up."

"I'll be right there. Care to join in?" She directed the question at Logan and was pleased when he reached for his crutches.

"May as well, since I won't be running any marathons with these things." He tucked them under his arms and followed her out of the office into the evidence room, where Sparks had set up her minilab.

"Great job," she commented as they filed into the room. "You must have had some forensic training."

"A little. Nothing major, but enough to keep our conviction rate up."

Logan hobbled into the room and leaned his crutches up against the doorjamb. He'd had to demand a walking cast, which the doc had reluctantly given him. Without one, it would have been impossible to do his job with any efficiency.

He watched Rory pull latex gloves from the dispenser and put them on. She'd followed in her dad's meticulous footsteps, a good move, he decided, as he watched her pick up the skull and begin her examination.

She sat it down under an intensely bright light and picked up her camera. Moving in close, she snapped several pictures from different angles.

"Oh, my gosh." He watched her tense and straighten up.

"What?" he asked, his curiosity pricked.

She put the camera down and picked up the skull. Her hands shaking.

"Dammit, Rory. What's going on?" he asked, searching her face for clues.

"Do you have a rubber-cast kit?"

"Yes," Sparks said.

"I need it." She moved to the microscope and detached the deck before setting the skull under the scope.

"I'll get it. It's in my rig." Sparks strode from the room.

"I missed these two marks on the forehead. They're deep and weatherworn."

Logan held his concern at bay while he watched her put her eye to the lens and adjust the magnification.

A tiny gasp escaped from between her lips, setting his nerves on edge. "Out with it."

She pulled back and grasped the edge of the table. "Did the victim this morning have any kind of marks on her forehead?"

"You mean, besides scrapes and bruises?"

"Yes. They'd be very distinct, straight cut marks down to the bone."

"Seven. There were seven of them. Clear across her forehead. Is that significant?"

"Yeah. This skull has two marks cut into it."

Logan hobbled toward her. "Let me see."

She stepped aside and let him stare into the eyepiece, where the powerful microscope highlighted two cut marks, deep into the bone, approximately half-an-inch long and half-an-inch apart.

He straightened and pulled back. "What do they mean?"

The color left her face and he braced for the revelation he instinctually knew would rock his world, because it had already shattered hers.

"I've seen these marks before. In the case I'm working in Los Angeles. We've got a serial who marks his victims just like this."

"Do you think it's the same guy?"

"I won't know for certain until I take an impression of the marks for comparison, but, yeah, I think it's him."

Caution slicked his nerves as he considered the information.

"It's a detail we withheld from the press. Only the killer and those close to the investigation know about it."

Rage chased through him as he pulled her into his arms. The blindfold, the way the hands were tied all matched the M.O. on the dead girl to the M.O. in her attack. The cut marks matched the Los Angeles serial's M.O. It couldn't be any clearer if it had been spelled out.

They were dealing with the same psychopath, but had he followed Rory to L.A., or had she been forced to return to his killing grounds?

"Here's the casting kit." Sparks came back into the room.

Rory pulled away from Logan. "Thanks."

He brought it around the table and handed it to her.

She swallowed the fear that seemed to radiate from somewhere deep in her chest, filling her mind with unshakable foreboding.

She shivered as she poured the powdered impression compound into a small mixing bowl and added a couple teaspoons of water.

If the marks matched, this skull belonged to his second victim. The Los Angeles victims had been numbered four and five, if the marks were indicative of a victim number—and she didn't have any evidence to refute the assumption. Forensic dating put their murders sometime during the month of May. The killer's time line was spread over four or more years, if the link held up.

Stirring the mixture until it was smooth, she scooped some out on a wooden tongue depressor and forced it into the marks on the skull, careful to dispense it evenly and with enough pressure to fill every crack and crevice.

"Three minutes." She stepped back, flinching when she bumped into Logan. The contact seared her, but she fought the urge to pull away. Instead, she hung on through the burn until it subsided. She'd managed to avoid physical contact with the opposite sex since her attack. It was better that way.

Safer.

"I'll call the medical examiner. Have him take a close look at the imprint marks on the woman we found today."

His breath was warm against her ear. She let the pleasurable sensation still her nerves. He had always touched her in a slow, seductive way. How she'd ever let a madman's degradation of her erode what they had seemed ridiculous now.

She shuddered as he stepped back, instantly missing the closeness.

Her attacker hadn't raped her, thank God. But his physical savagery and control had left her broken.

"That should do it," Sparks said, looking at his watch.

She glanced up at the deputy. "I'll pull it. Then we'll take another one for the L.A. lab."

Carefully, she lifted a corner of the mold and

peeled it off the skull, before examining it to make sure it was complete. "Looks good. We'll ship it out with the other bones."

"I'll package it up." Sparks took the impression from her and left the evidence room.

Rory sagged against the counter, spent. She had been running from this for six years, but it had come full circle. All these years, she'd thought she was safe hundreds of miles from Reaper's Point, but it was a myth as ludicrous as denying the danger-ous beauty that surrounded the entire town and its mountain.

She hadn't escaped fear despite how hard and fast she'd run from it. She'd only postponed it.

"M.E. Travis will pull anything he can get from the body and ship it to us," Logan said as he en-tered the room.

Even though the sun was shining outside and streaming in through the window, a dark shadow covered her.

Logan hobbled over to Rory, sensing her trepi-dation. "Hey. Don't let this eat you alive. You're not alone."

She stared up at him, doubt in her eyes.

He allowed a measure of her frustration to rub off on him. "I'm going to call in the FBI, just as soon as you've shipped off the bones. We're going to give this everything we've got, this time."

A tentative smile turned her lips.

He brushed his hand along her cheek, feeling his

desire flame up, hot and intense. If only he could forget the nights they'd shared together. If only the thought of the nights he wanted to share with her would go away, maybe he could move past it and just do his damn job. Find the maniac who'd stolen her mind and her body from him.

She pulled away and walked to the window, staring out at the mountain.

His nerves twisted as he stepped up behind her. Not too close, but not far enough away, either.

"He's up there, Logan. For all we know, he's watching us right now. Laughing at our feeble attempts to catch him."

Anger rattled through him. Anger and regret that he couldn't prove her wrong.

"He's just a man, Rory. Flesh and blood like you and me. Don't give him power he doesn't have."

He reached out, running his hand across her back, imagining the feel of her silky skin under his fingertips, but she didn't relax.

He stared over her head at the mountain that had taken so much from them.

Determination burned through him, igniting a pocket of strength he didn't know he had anymore.

He'd find the illusive bastard if he had to hike every square inch of Reaper's Point.

Chapter Five

Logan watched Rory pour the polymer silicone mixture into the casting box that held the skull.

They were a couple of days away from putting an identity on the killer's victim, but a hell of a lot further from any definitive answers.

"We'll need to let this dry overnight before we take the box apart."

"Then we've got time to grab a bite to eat."

She gave him a tentative look and pulled off her latex gloves. "Does Papa Roy's still make the best burgers in town?"

"He never stopped."

"I can taste it now. You know, I've seriously craved them since I left."

He knew what he'd missed when she left and it had nothing to do with red meat.

"Well, what are we waiting for? Let's get over there so you can reminisce with your mouth full."

She smiled and moved to his side.

Desire burned through him like blasting cord to a charge and he took her hand. "Thanks for agreeing to help with this case. I know how hard it is for you."

She stared up at him, tension working the tiny muscles in her face. Her jaw clamped tight. "I've got a huge stake in the outcome and if I don't participate, then my father died for nothing. He stumbled his way right into the killer's territory. I think he tried to get off Reaper's Point with the evidence, but didn't make it."

Logan moved in close to her and wrapped his arms around her waist, pulling her body next to his.

She didn't resist outright, but he could feel her hesitation. Feel her need to push away. She'd never described in detail what had happened to her on the mountain, but it must have been horrific. The madman had forever altered who she was and how she interpreted a simple touch.

"Yes. He did find something up there, and we have it, don't we? He concealed the femur bone until we found it. He didn't die in vain, Rory. He left us a trail of clues, knowing if someone looked hard enough, they'd find the answers."

He lowered his head, sucking in a breath permeated with her scent. An intoxicating mix of vanilla and clean skin. It was a scent he'd never been able to purge from his mind.

Rory closed her eyes, trying to keep from jerking away. He was so close, she could feel his body heat envelop her one searing degree at a time.

A shiver vibrated deep inside of her, but she stood her ground against the onslaught of negative connotations.

Logan had never hurt her. Never touched her in anger. She packed the thought into her brain and let it dictate her response.

She leaned back, coming to rest against his chest. Swallowing, she let his touch deepen. If only she could let him in. Let him physically express what she knew they both wanted to. But the fear was too strong.

With his touch would come control. Her body would no longer belong to her alone.

Fear, hot and irrational, seared through her. She jerked away, nearly tripping in her hurry to end the contact. She stopped short and turned to him.

His expression was hard. His eyes squinted in regret. He turned and snagged his hat off the counter, planting it on his head.

She searched for words to smooth over the rejection, but she couldn't find any. Her reaction to being touched had been primal and she regretted it now, but she couldn't let it go.

"Let's get over to the diner." Logan grabbed his crutches from next to the counter before moving past her.

She followed, intent on giving him an explanation, but the set of his shoulders and his tight-lipped mouth were barriers she didn't feel like breeching tonight.

Maybe tomorrow when she felt more rested, when the horrors of the day had a thin layer of time wrapped around them. Maybe then she could tell him what had happened to her on Reaper's Point.

Maybe.

RORY TRIED TO RELAX as they pulled into the driveway of Logan's condo.

Dinner, although it had tasted great and hit the spot, had been a test of her social skills. He'd become cool and distant, like the winter mountain snow cap. She didn't blame him. Rejection was a nasty pill to swallow, especially when it was administered by someone you cared about once.

Regret and guilt knotted her muscles until she thought she'd shrivel up and die. Maybe it was time to level with him. She'd spared him the details at the time—or had she just spared herself the shame?

She settled on the latter, realizing for the first time just how tightly she'd held onto the truth. Telling all would have hurt the people she loved and she already felt tainted enough without the added humiliation of exposing the details of her abduction and the madman's subsequent acts against her.

Logan killed the engine and sat back in the seat. He wanted to express his feelings and needed to protect hers. Whatever had forced her out of Reaper's Point six years ago was still there. Still driving some insatiable fear.

He reached for the door handle, but Rory put her

hand on his arm, stopping him. Hope surged inside of him as he turned to her, catching the sparkle in her eyes, illuminated by the porch light.

Did he see resolve? Was she softening slightly or begging him to leave her alone?

"I can't take this anymore. I want you like I've never wanted anything else. Hell, I never stopped wanting you. But I can't understand why you're holding out on me, why you won't tell me what happened."

She squeezed his arm tighter, as if doing so would somehow give her the strength to tell him what was locked inside of her.

"I—I don't know. I've held on to it for so long."

He took her hand, pulling it to his lips. She shivered as he brushed her skin. "I'm here for you... I always have been. So was your dad and your friends. Why did you run away?"

"I was ashamed. Ashamed of what happened on the mountain that night. Ashamed of the things he made me do."

"Good God, Rory! You were the victim. You shouldn't feel anything but anger for what he did. He stole you and did horrible things..." Logan's voice cracked. He swallowed the slice of pain that hacked into his emotions like a machete. He'd never forget that morning as long as he lived. The horror he'd felt infuse his body. The questions that plagued his mind day and night. He had the box of evidence in the case, but he didn't have her truth.

He had pictures of the injuries inflicted on her, but not the confessions of her heart.

Had the maniac taken those, too?

"Please, Rory. Trust me. Let me help you." He stared into her face in the dim glow of the light. A single tear slid down her cheek.

He brushed it away, feeling frustration cloud his thoughts.

She wasn't going to crack. Wasn't going to give him insight into that night. Not now, maybe not ever.

"Let's go inside. Get you settled."

She nodded and climbed out of the Blazer.

Disappointment caved in his emotional walls as he reached into the backseat and grabbed his crutches.

What secrets was she protecting? What had the bastard done to her?

Rage coursed through him as he climbed out of the rig and positioned his crutches under his arms. Maybe if he knew exactly what had happened to Rory, he could catch the man responsible. Maybe, in all the awful memories, there was a clue that could turn the case.

But until Rory decided to trust him with the information, his hands were tied.

RORY STARED INTO THE FIRE, enjoying the heat, even if it didn't warm the chill at the core of her being.

Logan plopped down in an overstuffed leather chair on her right and pulled his injured leg up onto the ottoman.

"Would you like a glass of wine?" she asked, watching him lay his head back against the cushions and gaze at her.

"I'm on duty."

"Duty?"

"Officer Taylor phoned in sick. He works graveyard and I don't have anyone to cover tonight. One of the disadvantages of being a small department."

Alcohol was taking the edge off her nerves and drawing her into a state of calm. Or maybe it was having Logan so close, so male, so armed.

She managed a smile as she looked at him, taking in his casted leg. He was a lion with a wounded paw.

"Thanks for picking up my favorite." She lifted her glass.

"You're welcome." He squinted at her and smiled.

Her heart rate revved up. "I'm sorry our discussion went nowhere tonight. It's not you. It's me. Being back here seems to have trashed my well-planned closure. I mean, I really believed I was past it, but seeing that woman this morning unraveled everything."

"You don't have to explain. You'll tell me when you're ready." He closed his eyes.

Rory watched the rise and fall of his chest as he drifted into a comfortable place. He'd be up most of the night working the graveyard shift.

Logan's portable police radio crackled to life. He bolted up in the chair, straining his leg in the process. Biting back a curse, he pulled the device from his belt.

"Belle County Sheriff, Belle County dispatch, do you copy?"

"Affirmative. What's the problem?"

"There's been a report of a prowler around the lakeshore—McCoy Drive. Mrs. Bulla Whitten reports seeing a man outside her bedroom window."

"Copy dispatch. I'll respond. Do you have a home address?"

"Affirmative. 512 McCoy."

"Copy. Zero-five-eight-seven-three clear." He put the radio back on his belt and slid forward in the chair. "Looks like I need to check this out. Will you be okay?"

"Yeah. I'm pretty tired, I'll go to bed and see you in the morning." She drained the last of the wine from her glass and stood up.

Logan came to his feet slowly and picked up his crutches. "The summer folk next door haven't left yet. Tom and his wife, Cindy, are good people. If you need anything knock on their door."

"Stop worrying about me. McCoy Drive is only a couple of miles from here. I'll sleep on the phone if I have to and I've got the .38 in the bedside table. I'll be fine."

He poked the crutches under his arms and hobbled to the door. "Lock up behind me."

She grinned at him, accentuating the rosy flush in her cheeks. She would be fine. He'd be gone ten or twenty minutes, tops.

"Go!"

He obeyed, limping out the door to the Blazer, listening for the decisive click of the dead bolt. It came almost immediately.

Rory leaned against the front door, feeling a slight buzz from the wine. To say she was a lightweight was putting it mildly. Her friends in the city had always accused her of being a cheap date. It would have been true if she'd dated at all in the past six years.

She flipped off the kitchen light and moseyed into the living room, giving the logs in the fireplace a quick stir before she shut the fireplace screen and wandered down the hall to her room. Once inside she closed the door.

Tomorrow was going to be a decisive day. She'd remove the skull from its casting bed. Once she had the mold, she'd fill it with clay slip to produce an exact replica of the original skull.

Once the tissue depth markers were in place, she'd be able to feed the modeling clay into the press and layer it over the model.

She loved her job, she decided as she undressed and pulled on her nightgown. Sliding in between the covers, she turned off the bedside lamp.

Rory rolled onto her back, feeling content for the first time since she'd arrived back in Reaper's Point. It was probably the glass of Chenin Blanc she'd guzzled, but she didn't care. She liked the comfortable numbness coaxing her body and mind into oblivion.

She closed her eyes and welcomed the darkness.

LOGAN PULLED ONTO MCCOY DRIVE, shining his spotlight into the trees as he crept along the road. Prowler calls were pretty common around the lakefront properties, but very few of them ever amounted to anything serious. Usually a nosy neighbor checking to see if the lights belonged to the owners of the property.

Sweeping the spotlight forward, he looked for anyone on the street. Nothing.

He'd have to roll down Bulla Whitten's driveway to speak with her and make sure everything was okay.

He spotted the ornate mailbox with the numbers 512 on it and turned into the drive. Easing forward, he maneuvered the sloped entrance and pulled up next to the house.

If Bulla was inside, she'd gone to bed. The place was dark, an unusual happening in his estimation, since her neighbors constantly complained that she always left her yard light on at night, interfering with their stargazing.

Caution inched along his spine, setting his nerves on edge.

He knew Bulla Whitten. If she'd made a prowler call, every light in the house would be on. She'd be standing on the front porch with a loaded shotgun ready to blast first and ask questions later.

What if she hadn't made the call?

Logan jammed the gearshift into Reverse and backed into the turn around.

Popping the rig into Drive, he hit the gas. He'd fallen for someone's ploy, he only hoped it was a prank call.

He maneuvered the driveway, but by the time he reached the entrance it was too late.

Bang! The Blazer shook violently.

He slammed on the brakes, put the rig in Park and jumped out.

How could he have missed the strip of tread needles laying across the driveway opening?

He'd been drawn here. Deliberately called away. *But why?*

"Rory!"

"RORY. I'm here."

The whisper tickled in her ear as she drifted in the twilight between sleep and wakefulness.

"I've come for you."

Again the haunting voice raked over her eardrums, its timbre more pronounced this time, more alive and…

In an instant, the sound of his voice registered in her mind. She startled awake, breathing heavy, trying to decide if the voice was real or a figment of a vivid nightmare.

Sitting up, she stared into the darkness, her mind awake, her hearing on full alert, but only the pounding of her heart broke the stillness around her.

A shudder grazed her skin as her eyes adjusted in the dark. She peered into the shadowy corners of the room. Nothing.

Had she dreamed the sound of her abductors voice? God only knew the number of times he'd violated her headspace, waking and sleeping.

She lay back against the pillow and closed her eyes, wishing Logan was next to her in the empty bed, taking her into his arms. Soothing her to sleep in the protective circle of his body.

"I'm here for you, Rory."

Terror slammed into her brain as a hand slapped a piece of duct tape over her mouth before she could scream.

Her eyes flew open, but there was only blinding darkness around her.

Fear, debilitating and deadly, infused her body as he pulled her arms in front of her. The horror of that night six years ago came crashing down on her, as he tied her wrists.

She tried to make out his features, tried to catch a glimpse of him, but it was too dark.

Then came the blindfold.

He put it over her eyes and pulled it tight behind her head.

Rory's stomach rolled, a combination of fear and determination swirled inside her mind as he pulled her up off of the bed with one hand.

"You're my number-one girl."

She fought the urge to puke and lashed out at him with her legs.

Kicking in the direction of his voice, her bare foot made contact with his body, eliciting a groan.

"I like a fight."

Terror coated her nerves as she lunged forward, determined he wouldn't take her this time. Determined to never be taken again.

He shoved her. His fingers digging into her back.

She felt herself falling, but falling where? Which way? She tried to get her bearings in the room, but couldn't.

Stretching her arms as far out as she could, she braced for the impact.

Thud!

Blinding pain shot into her head followed by the gut-wrenching knowledge she'd hit the night-stand next to the bed.

Blood trickled down her temple as she lay perfectly still on the floor.

Was he still in the room? She listened intently.

Would he believe she was unconscious and leave, or would he finish the crime and kill her?

The questions ran together in her brain as she fought the turmoil in her belly and darkness consumed her. But not before she felt his hands on her skin and the tug of her body being dragged across the floor.

"SLOW DOWN, MAN!"

Logan stepped on the gas pedal harder and slid around the corner, ignoring the freaked-out owner of the vehicle he'd commandeered. The nearest backup cop to the scene was a state trooper eighteen mile away. He'd had no choice but to flag down the motorist and jump in.

"Someone's in trouble. Hang on!"

Logan braked, whipped around the last turn before his condo and screeched to a halt in the driveway.

Grabbing his crutches, he bailed out of the car and did a running hobble to the front door, hitting the doorbell several times before shoving his key into the lock.

"What's going on?" Tom Jenkins stepped out of his front door onto their shared front porch, dressed in his robe.

"Go back inside. There might be someone in my house. He could be armed." Logan shoved the door open, leaned his crutches against the wall and pulled his pistol.

Tom ducked back inside his front door, but stared out through a two-inch crack. "Can I call anyone?"

"No. There's a trooper on the way." Logan stepped inside the door, listening for sounds of an intruder.

The fire had died to a pile of embers, casting a radiant glow that sent odd shadows dancing across the walls.

He moved forward, his thoughts riddled with questions.

Was he too late? Had the skillful killer come to take the one who'd gotten away?

Fear twisted his gut into knots as he moved past the kitchen, through the living room and down the hall, afraid of what he would find.

A lump lodged in his throat as he paused next to her bedroom door. It stood open.

Reaching around, he found the light switch and flicked it on, aiming into the room with his pistol.

It was empty.

Terror laced through him. He stepped back into the hall.

The bathroom door was open. He glanced inside before flipping on the light. Clear.

Rage and determination coursed through his body as he approached the master bedroom. There was a sliding-glass door that led out into the back-yard and the field beyond.

If the killer had been able to get her through the field… He burned at the thought.

Logan stepped into the master suite and hit the light switch.

The slider was wide-open, the drapes flipping in the chilly breeze coming in through the door.

Then he heard it, a moan. Soft and low, muted in the darkness outside.

Bolting to the door, he raised his gun and

stepped out, listening for the sound again. "Rory? Talk to me, babe. Where are you?"

His eyes adjusted in the darkness as he peered out toward the field at the end of the lawn.

A dark form lay at the edge, just barely visible in the tall grass.

Stumbling forward, Logan hobbled toward her and collapsed on the ground next to her.

"Rory?"

A moan rumbled in her throat. He reached for the strip of duct tape on her mouth. It was evidence, but it was more important to hear her voice.

He peeled it back, listening to her suck in a deep breath through her mouth.

"I'm sorry. I never should have left you alone."

He pulled off the blindfold.

She stared up at him, her eyes sparkling in the scant light coming from Tom's back porch.

"I'm okay. Help me up?"

He swallowed. He wanted to pull her to her feet and check her over from head to toe with his bare hands, but she was covered in evidence. Evidence he'd need to catch the bastard.

"I'd love to honey, but you're evidence."

A gasp escaped from between her lips and his heart dropped. "Once the trooper gets here, I'll process the scene. What can you tell me?"

"That he was in my room. That I heard him whisper in my ear while I slept."

A torrent of anger swept Logan up in its grasp,

squeezing his heart until he couldn't breathe. "He must have picked open the slider in the master or…" He didn't enjoy speculation, he preferred facts. "Maybe he was in the house before we got home."

Caution sluiced in his veins as he reached out to touch her cheek. "What happened to your head?"

"I fought back. The nightstand won."

He suppressed a smile. "Hardwood always wins, darlin'."

"To hell with hardwood, get me up!"

Reaching out, he helped her come to a sitting position and rocked back onto his butt. "What did he say to you?"

"He told me I was his number-one girl."

The words pounded a warning deep in Logan's brain. "Anything else?"

"He told me he'd come for me."

"Sick bastard." Logan tried to brush off the foreboding coating his nerves, but he couldn't. The killer was here in Reaper's Point, hell, maybe he always had been. And he was a bold piece of… Walking into his home with the intention of taking Rory, again.

The flash of lights signaled the arrival of the ambulance.

"Please tell me you didn't call EMS."

"Oh, but I did. And from the look of the bump on your head, it's a good thing, too."

He brushed her back with his hand and made a silent vow. He'd never leave her alone again.

Chapter Six

Rory stared long and hard at the three photos in front of her on the counter of the evidence room. A knot coiled in her stomach and wouldn't relent.

The way her hands had been tied last night, matched those of the woman they'd found in the Clear Creek drainage and...the pictures from her abduction five years earlier.

She let out a sigh and straightened, watching Logan hobble into the room, minus his crutches. "Anything on the duct tape?" she asked.

"Nothing. This guy doesn't like to leave much behind."

"Probably because he knows it will help us find him."

Logan pulled up short and leaned against the counter. She was struck by his casual stance, but she could see a muscle work in his jaw as he crossed his arms and studied her.

"How about your L.A. cases? Any matchups?"

"I'm not privy to all the details. The information I have came from the detectives on the cases. I haven't seen the victims' photos. But I do know they were both tied up and blindfolded and that they had duct tape over their mouths. There are indications he took trophies, jewelry items, but the families weren't positive."

"Like your necklace?"

"Yes."

"But he didn't use tape on you?"

Rory felt the air push out of her lungs as the reason for that inconsistency buzzed inside her head. She needed to tell him. Needed to reveal the detail, but the words stuck in her throat. She searched for the courage to tell him what she'd left out of her interview. A sick detail that still made her stomach turn.

"He did put tape over my mouth."

Logan pushed away from the counter and moved toward her. Movement that made her uncomfortable. "He stripped it off just before he stabbed me…so he could…kiss me."

Logan stopped in his tracks.

Rory watched him blanch. His features went hard. "He kissed you?"

"Yes."

"And that detail got lost in the mix somehow?"

A huge lump formed in her throat and she considered walking out of the room, but thought better of it.

Logan moved in close and put his hand under her

chin, lifting her face up to where he could gaze down into her eyes.

"That's a significant detail, Rory. You know how valuable information like that can be to an investigation. So why?"

His eyes were dark hunks of rock, his features barely masking the rage she could feel coming from inside of him and radiating through his fingers where they held her chin.

"It was disgusting and I was ashamed. I couldn't tell you. What good would it have done?"

He released her and stepped back. His shoulders sagged in resignation.

She brushed his arm with her hand. "Please try to understand. I just couldn't tell."

When he looked directly at her again, the rage had evaporated, replaced instead with a measure of sadness. "You have nothing to be ashamed of. That kiss was just another method of control. A way to build himself up in his own sick mind."

He reached out and pulled her into his arms.

She let his words soak into her brain. Everything he'd said was true. She knew it in her mind, had studied it in psych, but it didn't resonate in her heart. And what about all the other things he'd done to her? Things she was too ashamed to talk about. The way he'd humiliated her, dehumanized her physically and emotionally. Wasn't that control? His control over her body and mind?

Her cheeks burned red-hot as she remembered

that night's events in detail. She pushed back from Logan and bolted from the room, desperate for fresh air. Desperate for solace from the conflicted thoughts rattling around in her mind. She hadn't asked to be taken. She hadn't ever responded, had she? Not even to survive.

Logan took off after Rory, his heart pounding in his chest like a racehorse on derby day. He'd pushed her too hard. Pushed until she'd confessed to something that no doubt haunted her.

He felt like scum as he hobbled out the front door of the department, spotting her sitting on a huge rock at the edge of the parking lot, her back to the mountain.

Slowing his pace, he worked on the words he'd say to her. Words that could alleviate her shame, but before he reached her he realized that nothing he could say would give her back her innocence.

The heat of tears stung the back of Rory's eyelids, but she held them in, determined not to cry. She gulped down several deep breaths and felt her emotions cool.

Listening, she honed in on Logan's clip-clop progress across the parking lot. She wanted him to hold her. Wanted to dissolve against his chest and feel safe.

Safe from the unexpressed terror that bombarded her relentlessly. Safe from the madman who'd taken her twice. Safe from the knowledge that her father had been killed trying to find the truth.

Then Logan was there, next to her. The touch of his hand against her back was solace. He didn't speak, just slid in behind her, wrapping his arms around her waist.

Leaning into him, she closed her eyes, surrendering to the flood of emotion and desire that coursed inside of her and threatened to overflow.

She would have to trust Logan. She would have to let go of her fear and move past the blame. If she didn't, then the killer had won that day on the mountain.

She couldn't live with that, not now…not ever.

LOGAN WATCHED Rory work the metal spatula into the seam on the mold box and pry it apart. She laid the instrument down and, with her fingertips, finished pulling the mold apart, exposing the skull surrounded by molding compound.

Carefully, she jockeyed the skull until it worked free of the mold. Picking up a cleaning brush, she removed the remnants of polymer.

"You know your stuff."

She gave him a smirk, then smiled. "Duh."

"Just like your old man. A smart-ass."

Her eyes sparkled with defiance and he had to rein in the sudden and urgent need to kiss her. He'd always enjoyed Dr. Matson's sense of humor and his quick wit.

Rory was like him in so many ways.

"What next?"

"I seal the box back together using giant rubber bands and fill it with clay slip. It dries overnight and tomorrow we have an exact replica of the skull my father picked up on the mountain. I glue tissue depth markers on the replica and from there it's pure art. Glass eyes in the sockets and my best estimation of the nose and lip shape, based on cranial measurements and race."

"You're a genius, Rory Matson." He watched a grateful smile turn her perfect mouth and looked away. Holding her this morning had been an exercise in self-restraint, but it had seemed to help for some reason. Maybe she just needed human contact. A safe place to fall with everything going on around them.

"You can have a job in my department anytime you like."

Her smile faded. She sucked in a deep breath and put her head down, working the soft bristled cleaning brush over every inch of the skull.

"Is Deputy Sparks going to package this for shipment?"

"Yeah. Any special instructions?"

"No. It's already survived more than a couple of winters on the mountain. There isn't any evidence left. If my dad had found a lower jawbone with some teeth in it, we might have been in luck, but the skull alone is a dead end until I give her an identity."

"Do your best. I'm going to find Sparks to

package everything up. We'll get it out tomorrow morning."

"Thanks." Rory stared after him, a new appreciation simmering inside of her. He'd changed over the past six years. He'd matured into a man and she couldn't keep her body from realizing that fact no matter how hard she tried to downplay it. She'd been celibate since she'd left Reaper's Point, but she sure as hell wasn't blind.

"Hey. Logan says you're ready to have that boxed up," Sparks said as he strode into the evidence room with a long narrow box and a roll of Bubble Wrap.

"It's ready." She sat the cleaned skull down on the counter. "I'll get you the shipping address. My colleague Jonas MacCafferty is expecting it. I called him yesterday."

"Must be nice to have a lab that size at your disposal."

"Yes. It is." She moved around the counter and snagged the femur bone from where she'd laid it down wrapped in brown paper. "Jonas is one of the best forensic analysts in the country."

"Is that right?"

"He's forever being tapped to provide expert witness testimony at trials all over the country. His frequent-flier miles are to die for."

A shy grin turned Sparks's mouth. "Cool."

Rory wrapped the femur in a thick blanket of Bubble Wrap and laid it into the box. Next, she put the skull into a large brown paper bag and taped it shut, before layering it in the packing material. "Have you got the impression I took of the cut mark in the skull?"

"Yeah." Sparks moved to a tall metal cupboard next to the wall and pulled the door open.

He hunted the shelves and pulled out the casting. "Here it is." Carefully he laid it into a small cardboard box lined with cotton and secured the lid.

"You're pretty good at that." She gave Sparks a sideways glance.

"I'm all there is between evidence and trial. I took some training in Los Angeles in May. In fact, I took it at your lab."

"Really. I'm impressed. They don't let just any bonehead into the program."

Sparks grinned like a high-school freshman with a new haircut and a hot date. "Logan helped me get into the course. But I know it was out of pure frustration."

"Oh, yeah?"

"Officer Taylor was having a hell of a time preserving everything. So it made sense for me to get trained."

"Let's put it to work, Deputy." Logan stepped into the doorway of the evidence room.

Rory looked up.

His eyes were dark, his features grim. Her heart squeezed as she pulled off her latex gloves.

"What is it, Logan? What's going on?"

"They found more bones on Reaper's Point."

She took a step back toward the counter and grabbed it to steady herself. "Oh, no."

"We've got to go up the mountain again and I can't leave you here alone."

She searched his face, hoping to see some sort of compromise in his hard stare, but it wasn't there. "I can't go…I don't want to go."

"You have to go. I need you."

She swallowed the terror slowly spreading through her like poison. It took her breath for a moment and twisted her nerves in knots. "Where?"

"Some climbers working their way up the north face found the remains."

Heat surged in her body. She tightened her grip on the countertop. It was near where her father had died. Near where the killer had most likely taken his life.

"What about your leg? You can't climb." She watched his teeth clamp together. Realization pulsed through her. "No way. I can't do it."

"I'll be right behind you, Rory. I've got a four-wheeler for the steep places. It'll get me almost there. Sparks will go up with you. Search and Rescue is probably rolling to Base-Camp as we speak."

Logan read the fear in her eyes, but he saw her shoulders straighten and her chin come up. Hope surged in his veins as he watched her fight an internal battle that had taken years to amass.

"I'll go, but not without the .38. It's at the condo."

"It's on the way." He turned and limped into the hallway, a mixture of anticipation and concern driving him forward. He knew how hard this was going to be for her, but, dammit, he couldn't leave her alone.

RORY BURST INTO the bedroom and pulled open the bedside table drawer where the shiny .38 lay. She checked the safety before shoving the gun into the holster she'd just strapped on. She gleaned a measure of comfort with the cold hard pistol on her hip. A least she'd have a fighting chance if the bastard tried anything today. She would pump every round into him without batting an eye.

"Ready?" Logan stood in the door frame.

She turned toward him and smiled. "Yeah, pretty much."

"Rory." He stepped toward her, taking her hands in his. Her pulse jumped as she studied his rugged face, mentally tracing it with her fingers. He squeezed her hands and pulled her to him. She let it happen, willed it. Pressing her cheek against his chest, she listened to the strong thud of his heart against her ear.

"Your dad would be proud of you. He'd know how difficult this is and he'd urge you on."

"I know," she whispered. "Why do you think I'm doing it?"

His embrace softened and he tilted her chin back with his hand.

Desire, hot and urgent moved through her as she stared up at him, his intention as clear as a July morning.

He kissed her. Slow and easy at first. She kissed him back, enjoying the feel of his mouth against hers, giving her hungry kisses that seared her lips until she thought she'd go crazy with need.

Logan felt it, too, because he kissed her harder, drawing on the response she was compelled to give. A response she'd denied for too long. He hardened against her and she suppressed a moan deep in her throat. In a flash, fear bolted through her and she dragged her lips away from his, feeling torn between what she knew and what she'd known with him in the past.

Determined to still her fear, she leaned into him, until the rampant emotion subsided and the heat of the kiss cooled.

"I need time, Logan. Time to work through this." She leaned back and gazed into his face.

"As much as you want." He brushed his hand along her cheek, sending a chill through her body. She closed her eyes, absorbing the sensation like a sponge, only the crackle of Logan's handheld radio was strong enough to bring her out of the intoxication.

"What's your twenty, Sheriff?"

"My home. We'll be en route in five. Zero-five-eight-seven-three clear."

RORY LISTENED to the steady hum of the ATV as they moved closer to the location where the remains had been found.

Behind them on another four-wheeler, Deputy Sparks rode twenty feet back. Somewhere on the trail, her stomach had settled and determination had kicked in. She'd spent too many years letting her attacker rule her life. It was time to go after him.

She scooted closer to Logan's backside, letting the feel of his body against hers add to her arsenal of resolve. It seemed lame now that she'd blamed him for what happened to her, especially considering how elusive her attacker was, how murderous he'd become. A shiver skittered through her.

Logan rubbed her hands where they locked together around his waist. "We're almost to the end of the line. You and Sparks can out-hike me, but I'll be right behind you. Search and Rescue just left their staging area."

"We'll climb down. Sparks can get some pictures before S&R show up and I'll get as much information from the remains as I can."

"Good girl."

Logan's hand dropped from hers as the trail ahead narrowed to a single-file hiking path strewn with jagged rocks.

Logan stopped the machine, killed the engine and climbed off.

Rory followed, staring at the gear bag tied on the

rack of the ATV. She watched Logan undo the bungee cord and lift the bag off the four-wheeler.

"Ready?" Sparks shuffled up next to them, his gear in hand.

"As ready as I'll ever be." She looked into Logan's face.

A reassuring smile turned his mouth. "Piece of cake, Rory. You always were the best."

She returned his grin, feeling pride in her abilities. A talent she hadn't exploited since she'd left Reaper's Point, but it would return like riding a bicycle or hitting a baseball.

"Thanks. Too bad you have an injured paw or we could hold a little over-the-bank challenge."

"You'll get your chance, Matson. My paw won't be incased in fiberglass forever."

"You're on." Rory grabbed the gear bag and headed up the trail, listening to Logan's final orders to his deputy.

Damn. He'd gotten her onto the mountain again. The burn in her legs worked to reiterate that fact. She was climbing the steep trail toward the north face and it felt good.

Behind her she heard Sparks's boots grind against the rocks as he maneuvered over the rough granite surface. It would be slow going for Logan. He'd be at least twenty minutes behind them.

She sucked in a deep breath, realizing she was on the very same track as her father had been the day he'd died. The eerie thought rattled her nerves, but she kept moving. What had he been doing up here that day? He loved this mountain. Had explored it until he knew it like an old friend. He had to have discovered something his killer didn't want revealed and he'd somehow cornered him that day.

Rory pulled up short, her heart pounding, her lungs hungry for air.

Deputy Sparks pulled in behind her.

"This is a good place to take a break," she said, pulling her pack off her back and sliding her water bottle out of the side compartment. "I'd forgotten how steep this climb is." Popping the top, she swallowed several gulps before closing the lid and shoving the bottle back into its holder.

"You can say that again." Sparks found his water bottle and took a drink. "I though I was in shape. It sucks to be proven wrong by a mountain."

Rory had to smile. She was feeling the same way. This trek was more strenuous than an all-day workout at the gym. "This mountain has a way of taking you down a notch. The only person I know that wasn't affected by it was my dad. I think he was part mountain goat."

"He was a good guy. It's a shame about what happened to him. He was found at the jump point."

Rory's heart squeezed. "I saw the pictures. Some hikers found him, right?"

"No. Brady Morris found him and called it in from the Base-Camp parking lot."

A shudder wiggled through her. "He's Search and Rescue, right?"

"One of the best. I'd trust him with my life."

Rory picked up her pack and put her arms through the straps.

"Time's a wasting." She pushed forward, unsure why the information about Brady Morris stuck in her brain. She'd only met him once. The morning they'd found victim number seven and Logan's rope had snapped. He'd been nice enough. Self-assured. Not afraid to shut her down when she'd tried to gear up and go over the bank. He possessed some of the traits one needed to survive on Reaper's Point, but then so did a lot of other people who routinely scoured the mountain, rescuing others who'd overestimated their abilities and underestimated the mountain's power.

"Does he live here year round?"

"Nope. He's one of the boys of summer."

Rory leaned forward as she scaled a steep portion of the trail, knowing they were close to the jump point. Close to the place her father had taken his last breath. Close to where a killer had ended her father's quest for the truth.

"Where's his home base?"

"L.A., I think. His folks have a cabin here."

She knew the type. They blew into town at the beginning of summer and blew out with the fall leaves, taking more than they left behind.

"So he volunteers during the summers with

Search and Rescue, then spends winters in the city?"

"I guess."

"How long has he been on that rotation?"

"Let me see. He signed on the summer of your…"

The air between them charged, but Rory let it dissipate. She turned to face Sparks. "It's okay. You can say it. I don't need to be protected from it. It's just a word. Abduction. There, I said it for you. I just wish you and Logan would stop tiptoeing around it like it's a land mine."

Sparks held up a hand. "I'm sorry. I was following Logan's lead on that one. If you're not upset by it, then great."

She stared at him, seeing a flash of excitement in his eyes that seemed out of place in the odd conversation.

"I'm the one who should apologize. I didn't mean to snap. I've let the fear my attacker generated inside of me control my life. It's time to move past it. Get some closure."

"Sounds like a plan, Rory."

There was that brief spark of excitement in his eyes again. She turned and started back up the trail. Maybe Sparks had a right to be excited about her revelation. What law-enforcement officer didn't find a measure of peace in knowing a victim had finally met with some closure. She was entitled to that happy feeling, too, but it wasn't there. There was only the knowledge that her abductor was still out here and she was traipsing around on his killing grounds.

Pulling the last section of the trail, they topped out on the jump point and came to a stop. Her hands slicked, her mouth went dry as she looked around the small patch of earth surrounded by massive white pines five feet in diameter.

Which one had her father tied off to? Which massive trunk had bore the snap of weight as he'd hit the end of the rope?

"Let's get moving. We can't let those S&R boys have all the fun."

Sparks smiled and pulled off his pack. "You got that right."

Rory followed suit, pulling out her gear and laying it out on the ground. "Be sure you check your rope. We don't want another officer in a cast."

"That was a freak deal. Logan inspected his rope routinely."

"Who had access to his equipment?"

Sparks pulled on his seat harness. "Lots of personnel. The Sheriff's Department, EMS, Search and Rescue."

His answer didn't make her feel better. It was time for her and Logan to put their heads together and consider the possibility that the instigator of his accident might be home grown.

She slipped on her seat harness and buckled it, watching Sparks secure his carabiners to the metal loops on his harness, aware that he alternated the openings of the metal attachment devices, not an amateur move.

"You been climbing long?"

"Since I joined the department, about three years ago."

Rory clipped her carabiners onto her harness and picked up six tapers, then slipped them onto a biner on her harness. They were the stuff safety was made of. Small steel wedges with a loop of cable through them. Once fitted into the large end of a crack in the rock and pulled down, they held like iron.

"Have you rappelled the north face very often?"

"Are you kidding? I did most of my training here."

"So you're familiar with Reaper's Ledge?" Rory asked.

"Yeah. That's where the remains are supposed to be."

She was familiar with the sickle-shaped out-cropping that had contributed to the mountain's name. It was a common resting place one quarter of the way down before one rappelled three-hundred feet to the foot of the cliff face. A final hoorah of sorts, a place to change your mind, something she'd never done.

An ounce of adrenaline surged in her body, bolstering tiny impulses of excitement that pulled her nerves tight and heightened her senses.

She uncoiled her rope. Slipping it through her left hand, she pulled it with her right. Feeling its surface, feeling for any imperfections that could generate disaster.

She came to the end and looked up to find Sparks studying her. "It's good."

"Mine, too."

"Let's go." Rory pulled a sling out of her pack, a one-inch-by-twelve-foot circle of nylon webbing, and picked up her climbing rope. Together they each headed for a tree.

She wrapped the webbing around the tree trunk and pulled one end through, creating a loop. Popping two locking carabiners off her harness, she slipped them onto the loop, openings opposed. Next she tied the end of her rope in a figure-eight follow-through knot and slipped the loop onto the carabiners before giving it a firm tug.

"Looks good." It was the procedure her father had taught her. More like drilled into her head. If you wanted to come home alive, you always did it right.

She watched Sparks finish his tie off, then backed toward the lip of the cliff, pulling her rope as she went. The moment of truth was at hand, she thought as she clipped a locking carabiner into the loop on the front of her harness. Next, she looped her rope around a figure-eight descender, an eight-shaped hunk of metal, and clipped it onto the biner. Lastly, she put on her climbing helmet and a pair of gloves.

"Here take this walkie-talkie." She dug into her pack and pulled out one of the two short-range communication devices her father had always insisted they carry.

"You rappel first, get a look at the remains and call back up to me," Sparks said as he clipped the walkie-talkie onto his belt.

"Are you sure?"

"Yeah, you're the bone expert. I'll hang here. Wait for your transmission. And, Rory...be careful."

She nodded at Sparks, grateful he was here, but wishing Logan was standing next to him. "I always am."

Fighting the fear lacing through her, she tossed her rope off the cliff and edged over the lip of the face, shuffling her feet over the granite as she let the rope slide through the descender. Easing back on the rope, she used her legs to push against the rock and shoved off.

She'd done this dozens of times and she anticipated the next spot she would contact on the rock face, letting the rope slide through her hands before grasping it tight to slow her descent.

The force brought her back into the face. Extending her legs, her feet contacted the wall. She paused, gazing up at the ten-foot section she'd just rappelled. It was a straight drop from here—once she made it over the lip. She sucked in a deep breath and stared down at Reaper's Ledge, fifty feet below.

The tenuous chunk of granite seemed out of place jutting from the sheer rock face, but even more out of place was the pile of bones resting on it.

Rory swallowed and refocused on her task. There would be plenty of time to analyze the remains, but not from a rope dangling over a sheer drop.

She released the tension on the rope, letting her body weight start the rappel. Braking, she eased onto the ledge and tied off. Pulling an anchor wedge from her belt, she slid it into a crack in the granite and clipped a safety line to it.

Glancing up, she let a moment of exhilaration take her. She'd done it. There was solid granite under her feet, she was safe, she was fine.

Pulling the walkie-talkie out of her pocket, she pressed the talk button. "Sparks. I'm clean."

"I'll be down in a minute." His muffled reply hissed over the airwaves just before his rope whizzed past her and snaked against the granite face, dropping in a coil on the end of the ledge.

Turning her attention to the bones, she shuffled to where the remains lay. There was no smell of decomposition. No tissue left, really. The only obvious thing about the find was it had been put there recently and the skull was missing.

She squatted next to the skeleton, examining the femur bones. The length and diameter supported her findings on the skull. They were looking at a twenty- to twenty-five-year-old female.

The bones that went with the skull from her father's backpack.

Caution inched up her spine as she raised up and scanned the valley floor in front of her.

Was this a taunt? The killer's idea of getting attention? Well, he had *her* attention.

She dismissed the creeping knowledge before it could intertwine with her resolve, but the information was more than she could handle. She needed off this mountain. Out of Reaper's Point and as far away as she could run. Right now.

But there was no escape. She had to face her fear. Kick its butt and make it home alive.

Where was Logan? He should have caught up to them by now.

"Rory!" The desperate tone in Sparks's voice brought her head up.

A jolt of reality slammed into her as she watched him plummet over the lip, terror on his face.

His face. He'd launched head first.

Fear knotted her muscles as she maneuvered to avoid what was coming.

Plastering herself against the granite wall she waited for impact.

The rope snapped tight.

Sparks landed on the pile of bones, scattering them like broken glass and spewing them off the ledge.

He was still moving, still rolling from the force of the fall.

Terror gripped her nerves as he flopped like a rag doll and vanished over the edge.

Only his fingertips were visible, bloody and gnarled as he clung to the edge.

"Hang on!" She reached out and grabbed his line. Her hands shook as she tied a knotted loop in his rope and jerked an anchor wedge from her harness.

Slipping it into the crevice, she slid it down until it went tight.

Pulling a locking carabiner through the loop, she slipped Sparks's rope into it, just as Sparks gave a yell.

His grip gave out.

His fingers disappeared from the ledge.

Chapter Seven

Rory anticipated the moment Sparks hit the end of the rope. Keeping her eye on the wedge in the crevice she prayed it would hold. If it didn't…

The loop pulled tight, stretching the rope like a rubber band.

"Sparks. Can you hear me?" she yelled into the steady breeze that rose from the valley floor below.

"Yeah."

"How far did you fall?"

"About twenty feet."

"Are you okay?" She held her breath, hoping his injuries weren't serious.

"I'm scraped and bruised, but I'll live."

"Can you climb back up to the ledge?"

"Negative. I'll have to wait for Search and Rescue."

"Okay. I'll back up with another taper. Don't move around down there."

"Not a chance."

Rory pulled another taper wedge from her harness and lodged it in the crevice just above the first one. She laced a locking carabiner into it, then through the loop holding Sparks above certain death.

She locked it shut and leaned back against the cliff wall.

"What happened up there, Sparks?" she yelled, but the wind picked up her words and blew them back into her face.

Concern rattled her nerves. Gusty conditions could slow a rescue. She closed her eyes, listening for Sparks's response, but there was only the whistle of the wind against the granite face.

LOGAN PAUSED AND SAT DOWN on a rock to catch his breath. The jump point was less than a hundred yards up ahead, but his leg was throbbing like a boom car on Main Street. He sucked it up.

The injured leg was worth it. He'd managed to get Aurora Matson on the mountain again. He was no therapist, but just the fact that she was here made him smile. She'd loved climbing. He'd watch the fire burn in her eyes, felt the excitement in her body after she'd maneuvered a particularly difficult face. And dammit, he wanted to have her back. Heart, soul, mind, body…

Through the trees along the steep trail, he caught sight of movement, watching as a man clad in neoprene and loaded down with climbing gear steadily moved toward him.

It took a moment, but he recognized Brady Morris, who pulled up short and took off his sunglasses.

"Sheriff Brewer. What are you doing up here?"

"We've got a crime scene on Reaper's Ledge."

"No kidding?"

"Human remains. Since you're here and Search and Rescue is en route, maybe you'll tag along?"

"Love to, but it's my day off. And I've got plans."

Logan studied Brady, watching him slip on his expensive shades and prepare to leave. He couldn't begrudge the guy a day off. He was, after all, one of the best the mountain had ever seen.

"No problem. I'm sure your buddies can handle it."

"Take it easy." Brady moved past him and down the trail.

Logan kept an eye on him until he vanished from sight then stood up. This area was saturated with overprivileged guys like Brady Morris. The upside was, they liked to volunteer for Search and Rescue, a tendency that provided his department with some of the best-trained and well-equipped personnel in the state, without trashing his meager departmental budget. That, he could live with.

Forging forward, Logan covered the last of the trail and hobbled onto the jump area.

Terror raced through him as he stared at the ropes tied off to two separate trees. One slack, the other pulled tight.

"Rory!" He shuffled to the edge, attempting to

see over the granite lip. "Rory. Sparks. Can you hear me?"

He waited for a reply, caution rasping his nerves. Something was wrong.

"Logan!" Rory's voice echoed against the rock face, thin but audible above the wind.

"Are you okay?" He braced for the answer.

"I'm good, but Sparks fell. I've got him tied off at twenty-feet below the ledge."

"Good girl." A moment of panic rattled through him. He had his gear with him. But what about his bum leg? Playing cowboy could get them killed.

"Help's on the way. Stay cool."

"Like I have a choice, Brewer!"

Logan had to smile. Her sense of humor was intact. It was one of the things he loved about her.

In the distance, he heard voices. Hobbling to the edge of the jump site, he saw the Search and Rescue boys climb the last of the trail with Derrick Mitchell in the lead. They spilled out on the jump area, loaded down with equipment.

"I'm glad you're here. We've got a problem."

"You need a piggyback ride down, Sheriff? Brute there can handle it." Brute? He was a brute, all right, Logan decided as he stared at the burly young man built like a tank.

"No, but thanks for the offer. Your mission has turned from a recovery to a rescue."

The good-humored grin vanished from Mitchell's face. "What have you got?"

"One climber on Reaper's Ledge who can probably make it back up alone and Deputy Sparks hanging twenty-feet below. Rory Matson tied him off to a safety line."

Mitchell pulled open his pack, taking out the equipment he would need. "No problem, Sheriff. We'll take it from here."

"Thanks." Logan stepped back, allowing the team to work.

Maybe getting Rory onto the mountain again wasn't the best idea he'd ever had, but her experience and know-how had certainly saved Deputy Wade Sparks's life.

Logan paced near the edge of the jump zone, trying to ease the tension knotting his nerves. He'd feel better when they were both topside and intact. He stared at the ground, wondering what had gone wrong. Sparks was an intermediate climber—good, but not the best.

Logan froze. His gaze locked onto a single footprint in the thick clay dirt. His mouth went dry as he knelt next to it, studying it closely, knowing full well where he'd seen it before.

The muscles between his shoulder blades bunched as he looked up at the Search and Rescue team, studying their boots, looking for the single brand that bore the distinctive tread pattern. But it wasn't there.

Coming to his feet, he resisted the urge to unholster his pistol. The bastard could be lurking anywhere. Endless possibilities for cover existed all around them. But he'd been there. Recently. And what about Sparks's accident? Was it possible the killer had something to do with it? There was only one way to find out. Fortunately, both of the witnesses were alive to tell about it.

Logan kept his senses on high alert, scanning the woods periodically as the team rappelled to the ledge below. Only when he spotted the top of Rory's purple helmet, did he let his guard down—and then only long enough to move in her direction.

"What happened?" Logan stared down at her, turned on by the gleam in her eyes, the slightly tousled lay of her hair as she undid the buckle on her helmet and pulled it off. This was the Rory he knew. This was the woman who'd been able to spin his senses around her little finger since the day he laid eyes on her.

"I don't know for sure. You'll have to ask Sparks. One minute he was saying he'd be right down. The next, he was plunging off the lip headfirst. It's pure luck his slag rope was on the ledge where I could get to it. Otherwise…"

"Could he have been pushed?" Logan watched a measure of fear bunch her face.

"Yeah."

He clasped her elbow and moved her to where the footprint was pressed into the dirt. "Look familiar?"

Rory's face blanched, confirming his assessment.

"It's him. He was here. He could have pushed Sparks."

With Search and Rescue behind him and Rory and Sparks ahead of him, there was only one person he'd met in the middle—Brady Morris. But he hadn't paid any attention to his boots.

"Easy…take it slow," Mitchell coaxed.

Logan turned in time to see Sparks make the lip, crawl forward, turn and collapse onto his back. He moved to where his deputy stared up at the sky.

"Rough one?" he asked.

"Kissing the ground comes to mind."

"After what you've been through, I'll bet. Want to tell me what happened?"

Sparks closed his eyes for a moment then opened them again before sitting up. "Yeah, but you're not going to like it."

"I'm listening."

"Someone shoved me from behind. I was geared up and about to rappel down."

"Did you get a look at him?"

"No. Nothing. I was focused on my line of descent. I never even heard the bastard come up behind me."

Logan extended his hand and helped Sparks to his feet. "I want you to go in and get checked over. Make sure you're okay. Take a couple of days off, you're going to be sore."

"I'm fine, Logan, really." Deputy Sparks straightened and walked to where Mitchell waited to give him a head-to-toe assessment in true E.M.T. fashion. As much as Sparks claimed the opposite, Logan knew he was hurting. You couldn't launch off a cliff without some kind of injury.

He turned to see Rory standing close by. There was no doubt from the look of horror on her face, she'd heard the exchange. Knew that what had happened to Sparks was no accident. Knew that it could have been her.

"What about the bones. Were you able to get anything before Sparks fell?"

"They were the skeletal remains that go with the skull my dad had in his backpack, I'm almost sure, but when Sparks hit the ledge, he scattered the bones. I'm afraid they're at the bottom of the cliff face. We'll have to recover them from there."

"I'll get my deputies on it. It's gotten too dangerous for you to be up here and, frankly, too tough for me to be up here."

"I don't believe it. The invincible Sheriff Logan Brewer is human?"

"Yeah. But it's a temporary setback." He smiled at her, was glad when she smiled back. But even the brief play at humor didn't alleviate the caution coursing in his blood. They'd been within minutes of the killer, possibly just short of death, themselves.

"Come on. I need a shot of that footprint and then we'll get out of here."

"Sounds good. I'll get my gear."

He watched her move to the tree and untie her rope before looping it between her hand and elbow in a continuous coil. He'd have to do a better job of protecting her. He couldn't let her out of his sight, not even for a minute. From now on they were joined at the hip. That last thought made him smile as he pulled his camera out of his pack and trained the lens on the boot print.

RORY WATCHED Logan hang up the telephone. "That was Sparks. He checked out of the hospital. He's got a cracked rib and lots of bruises, but he's okay. It's a good thing he didn't hit his head."

"He didn't land headfirst, it was more of a tuck and roll kind of maneuver."

"Lucky for him." Logan moved to the couch and sat down next to her. The air in the room turned warm and she felt her cheeks flame. He was so close she could smell his scent in the air. She'd always had a thing for the way he smelled. It was something neither time nor distance had managed to erase from her memory. But there were other sensations, as well, that had endured no matter how hard she'd tried to forget them.

One by one they swirled inside of her until she thought she'd explode. Instead, she stood up and moved to the fireplace, taking a seat by the hearth. As the flames popped and hissed in the grate, she let a different sort of heat warm her back.

She didn't want to sleep alone tonight. She'd

known that this afternoon on the mountain and she'd been fighting it ever since. Knowing the night would come like it always did. Knowing Logan would be there in the next room. Knowing she wanted to be there, too. Safe in his arms.

"You did good today."

"You'd have done the same. That's what you're all about. Saving people."

"When I can." His face went hard, like a man standing at the gallows, waiting for a blindfold and final rites. "We have unfinished business, Rory," he whispered.

She stared at him, knowing the conversation before it was spoken. There would be enough explaining to go around, but would it heal the wounds between them?

"I know." She stood up and moved toward him, desire flaring in her as she gazed at the man who'd once rocked her world—until she'd abandoned him and ran like the devil had been chasing her. Maybe he still was.

"All this time I blamed you for that night."

Logan opened his mouth to speak, but she held up her hand, stopping him. "Let me finish."

He relaxed back into the cushions.

She moved closer, sitting down next to him.

"I understand now. You're human. I'm human. And we don't always get it right. Sometimes we suffer because of it, but that doesn't make it anyone's fault. He took me because he wanted to. Not because you didn't stop him. The blame is his. It always has been. I realized that today, clinging to Reaper's Ledge. The only thing I blame you for is not shaking some sense into me. And withholding this."

She moved into his arms, feeling them come around her as she positioned herself on his lap. Sucking in the surge of pleasure that accompanied his touch, she arched against him and lowered her mouth to his.

Heat exploded inside her body as their lips came together, but she felt him hesitate. Felt him refuse to deepen the kiss. A moment of truth between them? She couldn't blame him for being cautious.

She let the kiss end with a whisper-soft brush of her lips against his, then straightened, staring down into his face.

Logan had never taken their relationship casually. Was that residual style deterring him now? Or was there something she'd missed? Something time had driven between them?

"I'm sorry." She raised up off of him and stood, fighting the sting of rejection.

"Rory." He reached for her hand and clasped it tightly in his.

She stared down at him, struck by the look of concern in his eyes. "You don't have to explain. I get it. Maybe there's someone else in your life right now, maybe the way I treated you in the past has finally caught up with me and it's too late for you to forgive me."

He raised a finger to his lips. Her heart squeezed in her chest as he stood up, never letting go of her hand. Chills vibrated inside her as he pulled her against him and wrapped his arms around her.

"I know you're scared." His breath moved the hair near her ear as she melted into him.

"This is a knee-jerk reaction to the fear you're feeling. I could never take advantage of that…even though I'd love nothing better than to make love to you all night."

It was true. The evidence was pleasantly pressing against her lower belly. She fought a rush of desire that clawed through her like a caged lioness in need of escape. There was truth in his words. A truth that gave her pause. His protection was the only thing holding her together. His nearness, his brawn—it helped that he was never without his weapon on his side, either.

But what was she really after? Rory closed her eyes, remembering the way he had always consumed her body like a man on fire. His every move designed for the maximum level of pleasure it brought them both. An ache awakened deep inside her. She swallowed down the searing memories. Memories she'd blocked. Memories she'd let a killer's humiliation overshadow, eventually destroying the bond she and Logan shared.

Sudden tears burned behind her eyelids. She didn't fight them, but let them spill over, working to purge the terror, the anger she'd penned up inside. The feeling of helplessness and loss of control her abductor had imprinted on her mind.

"Let it out, babe. Let it out and don't look back." Logan's words pounded inside her head as the tears flowed until gut-wrenching sobs quaked through her, finding release within the protective fold of his arms.

All these years she'd been working toward this day. Toward this healing. It was only fitting that he was here. Encouraging her to accept what had happened to her and to move past it. To live again.

Logan's throat tightened. Silently, he cursed the SOB who'd hurt her. But it was nothing new. He'd been cursing the man since the moment he'd spotted Rory's battered body.

Gently he scooped her into his arms, cradling her like an injured child. He wanted nothing more than to love her again. But was she ready? Ready to let him teach her just how good they'd been together?

She'd stopped crying by the time he reached the guest bedroom and he pushed the door open with his foot. The yellow glow of the bedside lamp warmed the room along with his blood.

He carried her to the bed and laid her down, taking a seat next to her. Brushing his hand against her cheeks, one after the other, he wiped her tears as she stared up at him, eagerness in her eyes. Slowly, he traced her lips, beating back the rush of desire pulsing through his system, white-hot and intense.

"You're a hard woman to resist, Aurora."

A slow enticing smile turned her mouth. Did she know the battle that raged inside of him? The feel of her body next to his was exactly as he'd remembered it. But he no longer had only a residual fantasy, he had her, here…now.

"Then don't resist. Give in. I haven't been with anyone but you. After my abduction I couldn't stand the thought of being touched."

"I'm so sorry, Rory."

She reached out, taking his hand. "Show me. Help me remember what we had. Give me new memories."

Fire burned along his nerve endings, consuming the last of his resistance, reduced to a smoldering ache in his chest that extended to his groin and all the places in between.

He craved her body. The feel of her skin pressed to his, glistening with the perspiration of exertion. The indescribable pleasure of becoming one with each other.

Reaching out, he popped the button on her jeans and pulled down the zipper. "Are you sure?"

"Yes."

He helped her out of her pants and tossed them onto the floor next to the bed.

Peeling off his jeans and T-shirt, he stared down at her. His mouth went dry, his heart pounding as she sat up and pulled her blouse off. Reaching behind with one hand, she started to unhook her bra.

"Let me." Logan moved onto the bed, enjoying the glow of her skin in the lamplight. Moving behind her, he popped the bra clasp and slowly slid the straps from her shoulders.

She shuddered as he worked them down her arms. Pulling the garment off, he tossed it on the floor.

With a patience he didn't feel, he brushed her back with his hand. Her skin was smooth.

Gently, he moved her hair to the side, laying a row of kisses across the top of her shoulders. She was fragile. He could sense it in the stiffness of her body. As much as he wanted to rush, he couldn't. Not if he wanted her ever again. Not if he wanted her back.

"Relax. Remember how it was." He continued to brush her neck with his lips. Sucking in the scent of her skin. "I promise I'll stop if you want me to."

He felt her soften and she tilted her head to the side. He buried his face against her neck, staring down at the curve of her breasts silhouetted against the light.

Desire pulsed and throbbed inside of him, threatening to drive him crazy, but he tamped it down. They had all night to rediscover each other, but making up for six years of physical starvation wasn't going to be easy. It might take a lifetime.

Reaching out, he cupped her left breast in his hand, fondling her nipple until it hardened in his fingers. "I've missed you," he whispered.

A sigh escaped from her mouth as he teased her. "You're so beautiful, Rory."

He felt her tense, her right hand came up to cup his hand where it held her breast. "What is it? What's wrong."

"Nothing. It's me."

Sliding his hand down he rocked back against the headboard, pulling her in between his legs, holding her against his chest, circling her in his arms.

"If you're not ready, it's okay. However long it takes. I'll wait," Logan whispered.

She relaxed against him and he closed his eyes, shutting out the images of her slender body spread out before him. But she'd given him a glimpse into the torment her abductor had inflicted on her.

Logan rested his cheek against her head, reveling in the feel of her like he would never get it again. And maybe he wouldn't if he didn't catch the man responsible for tormenting her.

Rory tried to relax, to just let the moment be what it was. But having Logan so close was churning up things she thought she'd put behind her. Still, the words of her abductor sounded inside her head and she couldn't drown them out.

"No man will want you when I'm finished. When you've done the things I'm going to make you do. You're tainted. Do you hear me? I'm going to make you wish you were dead and then you will be."

The haunting declaration had terrified her and by the time his physical assault started she'd become numb. And there were other things she remembered. Horrible things. Things that made her stomach turn right now.

Gathering every ounce of strength she had, she forced the garbage from her mind, zoning in on the feel of Logan as he held her tightly against him. Their naked back and chest pressed together, the soft light in the room.

She closed her eyes, forcing the horrible images further and further back into her mind. She couldn't let this destroy her again. There was hope. And he was holding her now. Giving her support in the easy manner that he always had.

"Sleep here, with me." She waited for his response, dreading another rejection. After all, how much could he take? Men were wired to do the deed and his wiring had put him on the fast track tonight only to have the plug pulled.

"If it will make you rest easier, I'll do it."

"Thank you."

He smoothed her hair with his hand. "You'll have to wear pajamas or I'm out of here."

She smiled, understanding just how difficult it was going to be for him. "I'll drag out the flannels if it'll keep you here." She sat forward and climbed off the bed. Grabbing her blouse from the floor, she slipped it on before turning to face him.

"I could always trust you to keep your word."

"The night is young, sweetheart. Talk to me in seven hours."

Logan got up and picked up his clothes. His

theory had been proven. She wasn't ready. He'd be wise to keep that in mind the next time he let his hopes take off like a solar flare. But he was willing to wait until she came to him, really came to him with all the desire and readiness she possessed.

He slipped on his jeans and buttoned them. "I'm going to have a Coke. Want one?"

"Sure." She followed him out of the bedroom into the hallway, where he took her hand, giving it a squeeze as he pulled her to a stop.

"No matter what that bastard told you, or did to you, you're still beautiful to me." He smoothed a stray lock of hair behind her ear and smiled. "You can't let him control you anymore. You're the only one who can purge him from your mind."

Logan pulled her into the bathroom, flipped on the light and turned her to face the vanity mirror. "Put that image inside your head and keep it there."

He watched a myriad of emotions cross her features, as she went from skeptical to wearing a silly grin. "That's my girl. You'll get there if I have to drag you in here every morning and show you what I see."

"You're a good man, Logan Brewer. I don't deserve to be treated so kindly by you."

"You're wrong. You deserve it and so much more." He turned her to face him and raised her chin with his hand. Leaning down he kissed her on the mouth, asking for a response. He got one when she laced her arms around his neck and arched against him, returning the kiss.

Parting her lips with his tongue, he explored the sweetness of her mouth, which only churned up his barely cooled desire. Lost in the feel of her, he finally had to end the kiss and back up before he pulled her back to the bed.

"It's going to be a damn long night," he whispered as he killed the bathroom light.

Chapter Eight

Awareness prickled Logan's nerves. He opened his eyes in the darkness, unsure what had awakened him.

The feel of Rory curled up beside him was a temporary distraction, but he quickly squelched the rising need in his body and climbed out of bed, hobbling into the bathroom.

As it was, it had taken hours to fall asleep with her next to him. Dammit, his body had a mind of its own and he felt like he'd overdosed on a male-enhancement drug.

Closing the door he switched on the bathroom light and stared into the mirror, before turning on the cold water faucet and splashing the icy stuff on his face, though it really needed to be splashed below his waistband.

Something was up, he decided as he pulled the towel from the rack and dried off. He didn't know what, but deep down in his gut he could feel the coming storm.

The killer was here in Reaper's Point. Hell, maybe he always had been. But what was he missing? They'd never had a suspect in Rory's abduction and attempted murder because they'd never had enough evidence to link anyone to the crime.

The boot print was key. They had an established M.O. That was it.

Logan rehung the towel and rested his hands on the countertop, letting his head drop forward. They were dealing with an intelligent killer. He knew what moves the Sheriff's Department would make. He knew the ins and outs of police procedure. Could it be? Could it really be someone close? Maybe Dr. Matson learned the killer's identity.

They had to return to the cabin and pick over it again. Maybe there was something they'd missed. Something else the good doctor had hidden away. If they could only find it, maybe they could catch a break.

"Logan?"

The sound of Rory's sleepy voice brought his head up. "I'll be out in a minute."

"I smell smoke."

Panic shot through him as he pulled open the bathroom door and sucked in a breath of smoke-laced air.

"Get up! Hurry." Hobbling out into the bedroom, he pulled open the blinds.

Bright orange flames raged from the roof of the house across the street.

"Call the fire department! I've got to get over there."

Logan raced for his bedroom and pulled on a pair of pants and a shirt, before sliding his good foot into a boot.

His heart hammered in his ears as he tried to remember the last time he'd seen the owners of the home—the Rileys. Were they inside? Had they gotten out in time?

In the background he heard Rory on the phone, giving the location.

A moment's hesitation hit him. He couldn't leave her alone. She'd have to come with him.

Moving out into the hall as fast as he could with his bum leg, he caught her by the hand. "Grab some shoes. You're coming with me."

"But I'm in my pj's."

"What if this is a trick. What if it's a ploy to get to you?"

He watched her reason it out.

"My shoes are by the door."

Logan dropped her hand and moved to the table where his handheld radio sat. Snagging it from the charger base, he clipped it to his belt.

Rory'd already had the front door open when he caught up to her.

"I'm going first. Stay alert." She gave him a nod and followed him out into the night.

In the distance the wail of sirens raged as they

crossed the street hand in hand, but Logan pulled up at the halfway point.

The heat was too intense. He scanned the area for movement.

People were beginning to show up in the street. Searching faces, he looked for the Rileys—a nice young couple with one child—but he didn't see them among the crowd.

Concern jetted through him. If they hadn't gotten out early… No one could survive the fire that raged right now.

"Sheriff Brewer."

Logan wheeled around.

Laura Riley stood holding her infant daughter in her arms. Tears streamed down her cheeks and the baby's cries cut through the noise around them.

"Thank God, you made it out." Logan and Rory moved toward her, catching her before she collapsed.

Rory took the little girl from her arms as Logan tried to comfort the young woman who'd been his neighbor for only a short time.

"Where's John?" he asked.

Laura gazed toward the house. "I heard glass breaking. He made us go… I think he's still in there."

Horror washed over him as he pulled her into his arms to hold her steady, then gently lowered her to the ground where she put her face in her hands.

The first fire truck pulled around the corner and roared to a stop. The volunteer crew popped the side panels of the truck and pulled hoses out.

Logan saw the ambulance turn the corner and felt relief spread through him. Laura Riley possibly needed medical attention. Her child might need it, too. Turning, he expected to see Rory standing right behind him, but she wasn't there.

Panic zinged through him and his heart rate revved up. Where was she? Didn't she know how dangerous it was to be alone?

He listened for the cries of the baby. Nothing.

E.M.T. Michael Green jumped out of the ambulance and ran toward him. "What have you got?"

"Laura Riley. Her husband, John, may still be in the house. Rory has her baby girl, probably over at my condo away from the heat and smoke. You take her, I'll go get the little girl."

Michael nodded and squatted next to Laura.

Logan's nerves bunched as he limped across the street, every sense on high alert. Rory must have wanted to get the vulnerable child away from the heat and smoke. He settled his anger with that thought. But did she know the danger she was in? This whole intense scene could have been set as a trap.

Logan paused at the front door to the condo, listening for movement inside, but above the fire equipment across the street he could barely hear himself think.

Grasping the doorknob he turned it and stepped inside, again assessing the scene for signs of danger.

There was no mistaking the screams of a baby in distress, and the cries were coming from Rory's bedroom.

Quietly, he opened the coat-closet door and pulled his 9 mm down from the top shelf.

Loaded and ready, he progressed down the hall, hugging the wall, moving in silence. Was he too late?

The air caught in his lungs. He'd been too late that night on the mountain.

Sweat slicked his forehead. He pulled up next to the bedroom entrance. A slice of light shone from underneath the door.

Sucking in a breath, he raised his gun and booted the door open with his casted foot. Stepping into the frame he stared at Rory and finally at the .38 pistol she had trained on him.

He watched relief register on her face, before she turned the gun sight back onto a someone—or something—behind the bedroom door.

Stepping inside, Logan prepared for battle.

Laura Riley's baby girl lay in the center of the bed, still crying.

Moving with caution, Logan stepped into the room and closed the door.

Brady Morris stood perfectly still. His hands raised in the air like something from an old Western.

Logan's gut tightened. "What are you doing here, Morris?"

"Tell the babe with the gun to back off and I'll tell you."

Logan didn't like the arrogant tone in Brady's voice. In fact, he'd always found Brady Morris's arrogance more than a little annoying.

"The babe is more than welcome to aim her gun for as long as she likes. Now, what the hell are you doing in my house?"

"I saw the fire. I ran over from my girlfriend's place across the field to see if I could help. I heard a baby screaming like it was being hurt. I know you don't have any kids. The slider in back was open. I knocked. Didn't get an answer, so I came in to see what was wrong. That's it."

Logan studied Brady's clothing, a pair of boxers covered by a silk robe. Tennis shoes on his feet, no socks. His story seemed plausible, but he'd seen him today on the mountain just after Deputy Sparks had been pushed from the ledge.

"You can put your hands down. And get the hell out of my house."

For the first time, Brady was speechless and Logan felt a moment of satisfaction. "I'll have questions for you later."

Brady nodded and backed out of the room. "You know where to find me."

Logan let his shoulders sag, feeling the tension evaporate from his body.

Rory lowered the .38 and put it on the bedside table. She scooped the baby into her arms, rocking her to calm the infant's torturous cries.

He watched her, listening to the sweet voice she instinctively used on the infant, the maternal code women reserved for children.

His heart expanded, taking in the odd wave of

emotion that seeing her with the child evoked. Would she hold her own sweet baby someday?

Would it be his?

Closing his eyes, he forced the image away. There would never be a child for her if he didn't find her abductor, and soon. That was the only way she was ever going to physically get past what had happened to her. And he planned to be there when it happened.

The sound of the doorbell drew Logan's attention. "That's probably the mama bear. I'm sure she could stand to hold her cub right now. Make sure she's okay."

Rory smiled at him. A sweet smile. "She's so tiny. So innocent. I'm glad they made it out."

"Me, too. Now, let's get her back to her mother."

Logan followed her out of the bedroom and down the hall, then cautioned her to stay in the living room until he answered the door.

Glancing into the peephole, he spotted Michael Green and Laura Riley. He opened the door, letting them in.

Laura quickly strode to where Rory stood, taking the sleeping child from her arms. "Thank you. Thank you for bringing her over here."

"You're welcome. She's a beautiful little girl. What's her name?"

"Allison."

"That's lovely."

"She's named after her great-grandmother on John's side."

Logan studied the two women for a moment before turning his attention to E.M.T. Green. "Anything on her husband?"

"Yeah. They found him in his backyard. He made it out, but just barely. He's got burns on his hands and arms. Mild smoke inhalation. We're going to medevac him out tonight to L.A."

"Any word on the fire's cause?"

"Yeah. Riley claims a firebomb came crashing through his kitchen window at 3:00 a.m."

That was the same time Logan had woken up with a gut feeling something was wrong.

"So it was arson."

"Looks that way. You'll have to get the details from the chief once they get the fire put out and poke around."

"Thanks, buddy. You going to roll Laura Riley to the hospital?"

"Yeah. We'll make sure they're both fine."

"Great job," Logan said.

Laura paused next to him. "Thanks again." Smiling, she left the condo, her baby girl in her arms.

"Geez." Rory moved up next to him and he put his arm around her. "That could have been devastating."

"Yeah. They're lucky they got out when they did. Green said, John Riley claims a firebomb came through the kitchen window."

Logan felt Rory go rigid against to him before she said, "Do you think it was a diversion so he could grab me in the chaos?"

"Maybe. I think our killer might have done it so he could come in here and take you. Assuming you'd be in the condo and I'd be outside."

"What about Morris. He scared the hell out of me. I'd just laid the baby down and he burst into the room, wide eyed and scary. He was shocked when I pulled out the .38 and made him stay put until you showed up."

"You did good. There's something weird about that guy."

"What do you mean?"

"He was on Reaper's Point this morning when Sparks took his swan dive. He came down off the trail not fifty feet from the jump point. I don't trust him. I'm going to check him out."

"He would have had access to your climbing equipment, too."

"I'm not following you."

"Your sabotaged rope. Sparks told me this morning that any of the personnel at the station, EMS and Search and Rescue would have been able to access your rope. That puts Morris on the list of suspects."

"Along with every able-bodied volunteer in town." Logan sobered. Reaper's Point was loaded with service volunteers. It was hard to get his head around the fact that their killer could be one of his volunteers.

LOGAN WATCHED the last fireman close the side panels on his truck and climb inside.

Dawn was breaking over Reaper's Point and he paused for a moment to admire it. Somehow he never got tired of living in the shadow of the mountain. This was God's country. A place where the masses came to get away from civilization. Not where you'd expect a murderer to reside, moving inconspicuously among the town's inhabitants, mirroring, masking…surviving.

He clamped his teeth together and took Rory's hand. She was exhausted. He could see it in the flat expression on her face. Hell, he was right there with her.

The office could take care of itself for a while. He'd already called Sparks and told him he wouldn't be in until two o'clock or so. He'd grab some shut eye, but in his own bed. Having Rory next to him during the night had been anything but restful.

"Come on. I'm going to hit the sack for a couple of hours. You look like you could use some sleep, too."

"Sounds wonderful."

They started for the house, Logan turning the night's events over in his mind. It all made sense. A killer's diversion so he could grab his target. The fire chief confirmed John Riley's story. They'd found the remains of the firebomb container in the kitchen right where he'd said it would be.

Then there was the trespassing Search and Rescue jock who took a detour when he heard a baby crying in a house where there wasn't suppose to be a baby. On a gut level there was something about Brady's story that bothered Logan. He just couldn't put his finger on it.

Maybe he should sleep on it. Let his subconscious work the details. Right now he was too beat to even know his own name.

Logan opened the front door and followed Rory into the house. "I'm going to have a cup of coffee. Want some?"

"No thanks. I'm going to bed. Lock up." He watched her pull the coffee down out of the cupboard. "Now. Before I turn in."

She nodded, realizing they had to take every precaution, and proceeded to make sure every window and door in the house was closed and locked. Finally, stopping in front of him, she raised her chin.

"Satisfied?"

"For the moment. Wake me up around two. I want to go out to your dad's cabin."

"Why?"

"I'm not so sure we didn't miss something out there. Your old man was onto something and now that we have more evidence, it's time to take a second look."

"Okay. I need to pick up a few more things, anyway. We could go this evening."

"Good." Leaning down he placed a kiss on her lips and turned for the hall. Despite the desire the kiss stirred inside of him, he was too tired to demand a follow-up.

Logan entered his bedroom. Glancing up he suddenly remembered what in Brady's story was bothering him.

Brady claimed he'd come in through the sliding glass door in the bedroom. But after the killer had used it to try and take Rory, he'd put a wooden dowel in the slider track.

Limping forward, Logan stared at the track where the dowel should have been, but wasn't.

Caution inched along his nerve endings setting his body on edge. "Hey, Rory. Come here."

She poked her head around the doorjamb. "What is it?"

"Did you take the dowel out of the slider track?"

"No."

"Brady claims he used this door to get into the house. That means the killer removed the dowel, probably while we were across the street the first time."

"But it could have been Brady, too."

"Yeah." Logan worked the scenario in his mind. If Morris was the killer, he would have had plenty of time to gain entry into the house through the front door. He could have been waiting for Rory to return and planning to use the slider to get her out without being seen. But he had no way of knowing she would bring the Rileys' baby back inside and catch him.

"Something's not right, Logan. You saw Brady Morris. He looked like he'd just jumped out of bed. He had stickers on the hem of his robe and his girlfriend does live on the other side of the field. So you're ruling him out as a suspect?"

"I didn't say that." Logan stared at her trying to put it all together. "I'm going to sleep. When I get up, I'm going to bring him into the station for questioning."

"Great. I'll put a pot of coffee on at two and wake you up."

"Thanks."

She closed the door, leaving him alone with a knot in his gut and a tangle of conflicting thoughts in his head.

He undressed down to his boxers and pulled the drapes.

Bed would feel good, he decided as he strode to the nightstand, opened the top drawer and checked for his service revolver. It was right where he'd left it.

Feeling a little safer, he closed the drawer and turned to the bed. Determined to find some answers this afternoon.

Pulling back the comforter and top sheet, he sat down on the edge.

Click.

The tiny sound sent a rush of warning through him. He knew that sound from his police training, knew what it was attached to. If he moved a fraction, there wouldn't be enough pieces of him left to put in a casket.

The bed had been rigged with a pressure explosive.

He'd just set the trigger.

Chapter Nine

Rory stirred sugar into her coffee and put the spoon in the sink. She should have followed Logan's lead and laid down for a few, but she couldn't shake the anxiety working her mind and body over like a heavyweight boxer on fight night.

The sound of the telephone startled her. She sat her cup down on the counter.

"Hello."

"Rory?"

She recognized Deputy Sparks's voice on the other end of the line. "Yes."

"Is Logan around?"

"Yeah, but he's grabbing a quick nap."

"I need to talk to him. It's important. Can you holler for him?"

"I could, but I don't want to disturb him, can I take a message."

"It's about the woman, victim number seven. She's been identified. It's really important that I speak with him."

A measure of excitement pulsed through her. "Okay. Hold on."

She laid the phone down on the counter and padded down the hallway. Logan had turned in fifteen minutes ago. Maybe he wasn't asleep yet.

"Logan?" She knocked softly on the door.

No answer. He was probably already asleep.

She fought a moment's hesitation. But it was police business and it was important enough that it couldn't wait until afternoon.

She turned the doorknob expecting to see him sprawled in his bed sound asleep, but the scene in front of her sent terror vibrating through her.

"Logan?"

He sat perfectly still. Trails of sweat slicked his bare chest and dotted his forehead as he stared straight ahead like a fixated zombie.

"What is it? What's wrong?"

"Bomb."

The word came out as a whisper, but it's meaning screamed into her brain.

"Oh, dear God." She fought the urge to move into the room. "Where is it?"

"Bed." Again his whispered answer sent terror racing through her.

"Deputy Sparks is on the phone. He'll know who to call. Hang on."

She moved away from the door and raced back to the phone. Her hand shook as she raised the receiver to her ear.

"Sparks! Logan's bed has been rigged with a bomb. You need to call someone."

"No kidding?"

"He's sitting on it now."

"Tell him not to move. I'll call the bomb squad out of Cliff Side, but it'll take them forty-five minutes to get here."

"What should I do?"

"Stay the hell out of that bedroom."

The phone went dead in her hand. She replaced the receiver. Her throat tightening until she thought she'd suffocate. But she couldn't let the desperation of the situation shut her down. She had to keep thinking.

She walked back down the hall, getting her emotions under control. She'd be no good to Logan as a basket case.

Calmly, she stuck her head in the door. "Sparks is calling the bomb squad out of Cliff Side. Can you hang on?"

"Yes," he whispered. "Take cover."

The demand, even said softly, left her with no doubt of the seriousness of the situation. She didn't know much about how bombs were constructed, but she'd seen the results in the lab.

Fear coated her nerves and settled in her stomach, making her feel sick. The best thing she could do for Logan right now was to obey his direction. It could save her life.

"Be strong," she whispered, watching him shift

his gaze without moving his head. She expected to see terror in his eyes, but what she saw was determination. Determination to survive.

She gave him a hang-on smile and left the room. Her heart hammered in her eardrums as she made her way down the hall and into the kitchen.

Sliding down onto the floor behind the bar, she put her head in her hands. She couldn't let him hear her cry.

LOGAN FOUGHT THE URGE to move as though his life depended on it. He'd learned in bomb training that even the slightest movement or pressure change could cause an explosion. He also knew the bomb had been placed between the mattress and box spring so it couldn't be defused. It would have to be detonated in place.

His gut tightened. There was only one thing to do to curtail the risk before the bomb squad arrived.

He'd have to set it off himself.

The blast pattern of the device would be cone shaped. Spraying up and out like a land mine. Killing or maiming anyone above it. Timing and location were key.

Turning his head a fraction, he looked for the perfect spot to dive for.

If he guessed right, he'd live. If not…

Turning back, he closed his eyes, finding a measure of peace in the darkness behind his eyelids. Rory's face was there, too. What would happen to her if he didn't survive? No doubt the killer had been thinking the same thing when he'd walked into the house last night after setting the fire across the street as a distraction.

Maybe his whole intention was to murder him so he'd be free to finish what he'd started six years ago.

Killing Rory Matson for some sick, indeterminable reason.

Anger fisted in his stomach. He'd sworn to protect her and he would. He would if it was the last thing he ever did.

THE FORCE of the explosion shook the house, jarring Rory from her stupor.

Her blood went cold, her tears dammed up.

"Logan!" Jumping up she raced for the bedroom, afraid of what she would find. She couldn't lose him. Not now. Not like this.

Where the door had been there were only splinters of wood. Acrid smoke pushed out of the opening filling the hallway.

Rory pulled up short, preparing herself, if that was even possible.

The interior of the room had been devastated. Remnants of the mattress and box spring littered the floor, the dresser, everything.

She scanned the room for Logan, finally spotting movement where the end of the bed used to be.

"Logan!"

He fought his way out of the debris, surfacing like a diver coming up from the deep.

The air caught in her lungs. She charged forward and fell on her knees, wrapping her arms around his neck. She had to make sure he was real, feel his bare skin under her fingertips.

"Thank God you're alive. Are you hurt?" She pulled back from him, staring into his face. Memorizing his features as though she were seeing him for the first time.

"I made it, sweetheart."

Tears welled in her eyes but she blinked them away. "You're injured."

He wiped at a gash along his cheek and flashed her a smile that told her he was really okay.

"Couple of stitches. I'm good." He pulled her close.

Rory melted against him just as the doorbell chimed repeatedly.

"Looks like the bomb squad is a little late," she said.

"That was the second longest forty-five minutes of my life," he said, brushing her hair with his hand.

"Oh, yeah. What was the first?"

"Finding you on Reaper's Point, half dead, wanting to force life back into you."

A shudder racked her body as the memories reverberated through her and she finally realized just how much he'd tortured himself all these years. How much her abduction had affected him.

"I better get that. They'll think we both went to pieces. Stay here. You need a medic to make sure you're all right."

"Yes, ma'am."

She stood up, stepped over the debris and headed for the front door.

Logan pulled in a deep breath and let it out, trying to clear his lungs and revive his shot nerves. The gravity of the close call sent shivers of warning through him as he looked around the bedroom. The killer wanted him dead and he'd almost accomplished his task.

Voices and commotion from the living room focused his attention. Within seconds, Deputy Sparks and the bomb-squad leader, Hal Maccabe, stood in the doorway.

"I'll be damned. You couldn't stand to give us a shot at this one, Brewer?" Hal chuckled.

"Something like that. Now, stop grinning and help me up, will you?"

Sparks stepped through the doorway and came into the room, helping Logan to his feet.

He tested his bad leg. It still worked. Dusting the bits and pieces of mattress stuffing and wood off of his body, he straightened.

"Pressure device stuffed in between the mattress and box spring. Very effective if you want someone dead. I'll need anything you can give me, Hal. Maybe we can trace some of the components."

"You got it, Logan."

"Sparks. I want you to interview all the neighbors. See if anyone saw anything suspicious last night just before the fire at the Rileys's house across the street. Whoever planted this device did it after the fire started."

"I'll get on it right now." Sparks hustled out of the room.

"It's all yours, Maccabe."

The squad leader paused. "Glad you made the right move Logan. Guess that training I gave you paid off big."

"Yeah. Thanks, buddy." He slapped his old friend on the shoulder and left the room.

He'd shower and get down to the station. There was work to do and he needed to catch a break on this case in the worst way. They'd start with Rory's facial reconstruction. She was almost ready to give an identity to the skull her father had found on the mountain. Then there was Brady Morris. The only other person who'd been in the condo last night and his number-one suspect.

He knew he was in trouble the minute he entered the living room and saw Rory standing with her arms crossed, glaring at him.

"EMS is on the way. You were supposed to stay put. That was a powerful blast. What if you've got something internal going on?"

The only internal thing he had going on at that moment was the desire to take her in his arms again and make love to her until they both forgot their names.

"Fine. If it'll make you feel better, I'll get checked out, but they're not going to find anything. I'm not injured. Everything works. No concussion. No broken bones. Nothing."

She uncrossed her arms and moved toward him, an odd mix of serenity and bedevilment on her face. "So. You don't have a bed anymore." She moved into his arms.

"Looks that way." He rested his cheek against her hair, pulling in a breath of her scent. Desire, quick and impervious to suppression, laced through his body, making him firm in all the wrong places.

It didn't help that she was pressed to him like glue or that he couldn't let her go.

Sighing, she pulled back and smiled up at him.

He suddenly wished the house was empty, but backed off the thought when he remembered just how not over the abduction she really was. He could never take advantage of her vulnerability to appease his need, even if she allowed it. He wanted her fully and without reservation.

"I'm going to get cleaned up and then we'll head for the station. I'd like you to work your magic on the facial reconstruction. We need to know who that girl is."

"I agree. And we'll work on the sleeping arrangements later?"

"You can count on it." He turned her loose even

though he didn't want to and headed down the hall, his blood on fire.

"Logan." He looked up to see Maccabe eyeing him from the shattered doorway into his room. "You were right. From the pieces I've been able to find, it was definitely a pressure device. Rigged to go off when you moved or got up. Not an amateur job. It took know-how and balls of steel to slide it under the mattress. Your bomber had to be very careful or he'd have set the trigger himself."

"Any chance the components can be traced?"

"I'll do my best, but it won't be overnight. They'll go to the ATF lab. Could be weeks, maybe months."

"Do what you have to. I'm planning to catch the SOB before that."

"Good man." Hal turned back into the room to finish his investigation.

Logan headed for the bathroom to wash the fine layer of grit off his skin. He had to catch the perpetrator…now. His and Rory's lives depended on it.

Maybe it was time to consider sending her away? But would she go? Doubt chased the thought away. He'd have to do a better job of protecting her.

RORY WORKED INTENTLY, restoring the face of the skull in front of her pedestaled on a special base that put the work at eye level.

Smoothing the clay with her fingers, she worked

the last section into place, before glancing up at the clock on the wall. She'd been at it since before noon and the rumbling in her belly reminded her she'd missed lunch and now dinner, but the woman had a face. She'd worry about food later.

"That's it. Except for a wig. Let me get one from my kit." Moving around Logan she fished in the nylon bag containing an assortment of hair pieces, snagging a shoulder-length blond wig. Combing her fingers through the synthetic hair she straightened it and returned to the project, noting Logan's intense scrutiny of the likeness in front of him.

Careful not to displace the clay, she slipped the wig into place, finger-combed it in around the cheeks and chin, and stepped back for her first overall look.

"She was an attractive woman." A slice of regret cut into her heart like it always did when she completed a reconstruction. It made the victim real, gave them a voice. Sometimes the only voice they had. The only thing a killer couldn't take away—their identity.

"Gale Robins."

"What? You know who she is?"

"Yeah. I dated her."

The air pushed out of Rory's lungs as she looked from the bust back to Logan. He paled right before her eyes and she fought a sickening sensation in the pit of her stomach.

"Was it serious?"

"No. We went out a couple of times, had some fun. But I was on the rebound. She was here the summer after you left. Kind of a free spirit. That's why no one was surprised when she disappeared midway through the season. I assumed she'd decided to return to L.A. where she'd come from. But I was wrong, wasn't I?"

A muscle worked along his jawline and Rory felt some of his regret rub off.

"I'm sorry. She didn't deserve to die like that."

"No, she didn't, but I may know the last person she spoke with before she disappeared."

"Want to let me in?"

"She was dating Brady Morris."

A shudder quaked through her, leaving a chill deep in her bones. "He was in the house last night. He was on Reaper's Point when Sparks had his accident. He certainly had time to rig the bomb. And he had access to your climbing equipment."

"I'm going to pick him up for questioning. His record is clean. Not so much as a parking ticket. I've got nothing to base a search warrant on, just a lot of speculation."

She stared up into Logan's face, wanting to erase some of the stress she could see there in the pull of his mouth, the narrowing of his eyes.

Reaching up, she brushed her hand along his cheek. He closed his eyes for an instant and when he opened them again he trained them on her.

"Let's call it a night. I'm not a very good host. I've let you starve today. I'm sorry."

"Don't be. We can grab something from the diner. I just want to curl up on the couch with you and forget about this day."

His eyes sparked with sexual hunger and a warning hummed inside her body. The fire between them had been rekindled and threatened to turn into a firestorm at any moment if they didn't fight it. But she didn't want to fight it, any longer. She wanted to let it burn. But the middle of the evidence room was hardly the place.

"I'd go for that." Logan flashed her a sultry come-hither half smile and hobbled out of the room.

Taking one last look at victim number two, a.k.a. Gale Robins, she pulled a square of cotton cloth out of her kit and gently covered the entire bust.

"Good night, Gale. I'm sorry you were one of his victims. At least, we can return you to your family now."

Rory made it to the door, feeling an odd kinship with the woman who'd no doubt suffered as she'd suffered. The only difference was, she was still alive. The thought sobered her to the point of tears as she shut out the light and closed the door.

For now. But that would change if the killer ever caught her again. She knew it in her soul and it sent shards of fear deep into her heart.

He wouldn't miss again.

RORY MOVED DEEPER into the circle of Logan's arms, staring into the fire.

The chill that bombarded her senses wasn't the result of the temperature. It was more serious, something that wouldn't go away no matter how close she chose to move to the flames. The killer had set his sights on them both.

"We'll catch a break on this case, Rory. The bolder he gets the better the chances he'll make a mistake. And, when he does, we'll be there."

She closed her eyes, praying she could snag some of Logan's certainty for herself. She wanted nothing more than for the killer to be caught and punished for the horrific things he'd done, but she couldn't shake the foreboding circling inside of her; the feeling that the proverbial tip of the iceberg was the only thing showing. That underneath there was so much more. Maybe even secrets her father had discovered. Secrets he'd hidden away somewhere, yet to be found.

"Dad's memorial service is next week."

"I know. Several local businesses are planning to close for a couple of hours in his honor. Your dad was well respected around here."

"I'm glad he had so many friends. It kept him from being lonely." Rory's heart squeezed. The truth hurt. She'd been nothing but lonely since leaving Reaper's Point. What would her life to date have been like if she'd have fought her fears and stayed here with Logan?

"And what about you? Are you lonely?" He brushed his hand down her shoulder, pulling her closer.

"Yeah." Turning her head, she stared up into his face, wanting him with an intensity that took her breath away. She'd avoided human contact for too long. It was time to shed her fear and live again.

"I want to feel again, Logan. I want back what used to be between us. Physically...emotionally." Leaning forward, she stood up slightly and turned around, crawling back onto the couch next to him.

He leaned his head back against the cushions, his hand coming up to smooth the hair away from her face. His touch was warm. Solid. Reassuring.

"I'm a man, Rory. I'm always ready, but it's your heart I'm concerned about. This has to be more than a moment's passion. More than an experiment to see if you're over the trauma. I want you, but I want you to be sure."

She swallowed the lump in her throat as she leaned toward him, feeling his arms come up around her waist. She was sure. As sure as she'd ever been. Tonight she would make love to him. Tonight they would forget there was a killer waiting outside of the four walls surrounding them.

Lowering her mouth to his, she breathed him in as their lips met in a surge of emotion that annihilated the remnants of her fear.

Logan fought the all-consuming heat setting his nerve endings ablaze, but the feel of Rory's body only acted as an accelerant moving him closer to the fire that burned between them.

Her response was genuine, not forced. He pulled her onto his lap and breaking the kiss, he stared into her eyes. "I've waited six years for this. For you to come back to me. I'd almost given up."

Her lips parted in a sweet smile. Then she wet them with her tongue, a move that sent his desire into overdrive.

"I'm glad you're a patient man."

"I've got my limits, babe. Let's take it to the rug."

Her smile widened as she climbed off him and stood up.

They'd spent a lot of time and more than a couple of chilly nights curled up together in front of the fireplace.

Logan snagged the overstuffed pillows on the sofa and a fuzzy blanket and dropped them on the rug.

Rory was already working the buttons on her blouse, but he touched her hands.

"Let me," he whispered.

She pulled her hands back, giving him the pleasure of uncovering her a piece at a time. He undid the last button and took her blouse off, groaning as she closed her eyes.

The firelight touched her bare skin, painting her in warm flares and shadows. He unhooked her bra and pulled it off, exposing her breasts. She shuddered, her nipples hardening.

Yanking off his shirt, he pulled her close to him,

feeling her skin against his. Sliding his hands over her back, he worked his way around and unbuttoned her jeans, slid the zipper down and slowly pushed them off her hips. She stepped out of them as they hit her ankles.

Caught up in a desire so intense he thought he'd explode, Logan went to his knees in front of her. He hooked his fingers in her bikini panties and slowly pulled them down and off.

His breath caught as he kissed her lower belly, her skin soft beneath his lips, his hands moving onto her butt as he pressed lower, breathing in her scent.

Soft moans resonated in her throat as he pushed his tongue into her, finding her pleasure spot. He toyed with it until her moans became louder and more intense.

Rory succumbed to the pleasure arching her body. Reaching for Logan, she grasped his head in her hands as he explored her with his tongue. She felt her orgasm come up and spill over, taking her breath with it as pleasure racked her body.

He reached up for her hands, pulling her down onto her knees next to him, where he cupped her breasts in his hands, brushing the nipples with his thumbs.

She closed her eyes, letting the stimulation flood her body with desire so strong she wasn't sure she could control it. She reached for the button and zipper on Logan's jeans. The feel of his need excited her as she helped him push his pants down over his hips.

Timid at first, she brushed her hands over his chest, feeling his skin beneath her fingers. She wanted him with a hunger that couldn't be extinguished.

Memories of how it had been between them surfaced, sending her libido over the edge.

Going lower, she wrapped her hand around him, stroking several times, before he stopped her.

The hunger in his eyes was intense as he sat back, pulling his jeans completely off.

Rory's heart hammered in her chest as she contemplated what was to come. She loved the way the firelight played across his hardened chest and flickered over his thighs.

Swallowing, she spread out the blanket and stretched out, anxious for him to join her.

Together they lay on their sides, facing one another. She felt shy under his approving gaze and eager to explore his body with her hands and mouth.

He reached up to stroke her hair before sliding his hand along her cheek. "You can't know the number of times I've done this in my head. You're the best thing that ever happened to me, Rory."

Heat seared her cheeks as she stared into his eyes. "I'm sorry I ran. I just couldn't stay after the attack. There were too many disturbing memories here."

"I know, you did what you had to do." His hand against her face was warm, intoxicating. Turning into his palm, she kissed it several times before reaching for him.

She wanted to feel him inside her. Wanted the erotic excitement he churned in her blood.

"Make love to me, Logan." Her voice cracked as the plea left her lips.

His features hardened with desire about to be fulfilled as he pulled her beneath him.

Sliding down, Logan kissed her neck, working his way lower until he found her left breast with his tongue, tasting and teasing the nipple until it peeked in his mouth.

Her scent was all around him, pushing his desire to fever pitch.

Raising his head, he stared into her face as he worked her legs apart with his knee. There was no turning back. No line of escape from the pleasure he wanted to give her, one thrust at a time.

He would get her to remember what they'd shared time and time again. But it wouldn't be with words. It would be with action.

Rocking forward, he pressed against her. His pulse pounded in his ears as she opened completely for him. He pushed into her, sucking in a breath as the contact seared him to her once more.

Pushing deeper and deeper he buried himself inside her, feeling her wetness close around him.

"Logan," she whispered, pushing against him as he thrust into her again and again.

He watched her face. Kissing the smile on her

lips, breathing in her scent. Devouring her—a starving man at a table set for a king.

Waves of pleasure crashed inside of him as she tightened around him, reaching for release. Driving harder he pushed her to orgasm, his name on her lips.

He couldn't hold out any longer. With a couple of quick thrusts, he came into her, lost in the ecstasy that convulsed and sizzled through his body.

Satiated, he relaxed against her enjoying the feel of her body beneath his.

In the dying firelight he gazed down into her eyes, before planting a slow kiss on her lips. "Let the new memories begin."

Rory smiled. "And never end."

He liked the sound of that. Liked the thought of being with her. He pulled out and came to his knees, enjoying the sight of her body spread before him.

"I don't have a bed anymore," he teased. "Can I use yours?"

"Only if you promise to do that again."

"I promise. There's no other place I want to be tonight." He reached for her hand and pulled her to her feet.

Lifting her into his arms, he carried her down the hallway to the spare bedroom. Stepping inside, he shut the door on the world outside.

He intended to have her heart by dawn.

Chapter Ten

"Let's hope your dad left some sort of clue to what he found on the mountain." Logan glanced over at Rory in the passenger seat and turned off the highway, heading for the cabin.

"Something we can identify, anyway. It could be in plain sight. He did that a lot."

"Sometimes that's the best place to hide." Maneuvering through the only intersection in town equipped with a traffic light, Logan started up the curvy mountain road. He needed to focus on the case, but his brain wouldn't stop replaying the night's events with Rory.

He'd enjoyed every inch of her body, several times over, but had he mentally taken her back from her abductor?

Heat burned through him, frying his nerves. Catching the SOB was the only solution with any kind of finality. Nothing else was going to suffice.

"What do you mean, he did that a lot?"

"Doodling mostly. He'd fiddle with a pen and paper for hours. When I'd ask him what he was working on he'd give me some complicated explanation for the random drawing in front of him. I could never mentally turn it into anything, but it was there for him. We should look for an abstract drawing."

Logan sobered. He needed something to go on. Some link to Brady Morris. Not something abstract. "If Morris is our guy, maybe your dad found a way to convey that."

"Sounds reasonable."

"I need something solid to go on when I bring him in for questioning."

"I understand."

He gave her a sideways glance as he slowed the Blazer and pulled off the road into the driveway for the steep descent to the cabin.

Logan steered down the drive, putting his foot on the brake pedal for the first switchback turn.

The pedal went to the floor.

A charge of panic tightened his nerves.

Pumping the brake, he tried to bring the pressure up.

Nothing.

Grabbing the shift lever he pulled the transmission down into low, slowing the motor's r.p.m.'s. Again he pumped the brake.

Nothing.

The vehicle picked up speed.

"Hang on!"

Turning the wheel hard, he skidded around the hairpin turn. The front bumper ground into the embankment, sending a cloud of dust over them as they bounced out of the ditch and back onto the road.

"What's wrong?"

"No brakes." The color drained from her face.

He had to get the vehicle stopped.

Grabbing for the emergency brake, he pulled hard.

The SUV jerked several times, but continued its downward roll, picking up speed as the seconds ticked by.

Panic fused Logan's nerves. He could jam the shifter into Park, but he risked tearing out the transmission, the only thing between them and a fast ride to the bottom of the ravine.

"I'm going to run it into the ditch!"

Rory's eyes widened.

Logan focused on the next switchback, timing his bank into the curve.

The Blazer roared into the corner.

Logan stepped down on the accelerator, driving the rig forward. The acceleration pushed the vehicle into the corner, keeping it away from the steep embankment on the left.

His heart pounded in his chest. They were halfway down the drive. He had to reduce their speed.

"Hang on."

Whipping the wheel, he drove into the ditch on the right.

Tree branches slapped against the windshield.

Pop! The windshield on Rory's side fractured, shattering into a spiderweb pattern.

She yelped.

"Hang on."

Pulling the wheel hard to the left, he gassed up the Blazer just as the nose dropped into the ditch and caught.

The SUV spun in a one-eighty and dropped into the ditch, nose pointed uphill.

Still rolling, backward now, Logan yanked on the emergency brake as hard as he could.

The vehicle slowed.

Logan cranked the steering wheel hard to the right, driving the rear end of the rig into the embankment.

The Blazer jerked to a stop, throwing them both back in their seats.

Logan closed his eyes for an instant, letting calm settle over his body. They'd just adverted disaster.

He opened his eyes and reached for Rory. Taking her hand, he squeezed it, feeling her tremble. Near death could do that to you. And she'd had more than her fair share of it.

"We made it. Let's get out of here. This was no accident."

Pushing the button on her seat belt, he released it and undid his own. The passenger side of the SUV was plastered against the hillside, inaccessible.

Opening the driver-side door, he climbed out and helped her over the center console and out onto the drive next to him.

Sliding his arms around her, he pulled her close. "We'll get a wrecker down here. Find out what happened."

"Okay." Rory reluctantly stepped away from Logan, missing the contact. Missing the security she felt in his arms. He was the only thing standing between her and a killer who was intent on finishing what he'd started—any way he could, apparently.

"Let's head for the cabin." He reached for her hand, intertwining his fingers with hers as they started down the steep drive into the cabin site.

She tried to relax, tried to enjoy the fact that she wasn't at the bottom of the ravine, but unrelenting fear battered her harried emotions, cracking and splintering them a piece at a time.

She wondered how much longer their luck would hold out.

FRUSTRATION HISSED through Rory's body as she plopped down on the sofa, exasperated. "There isn't anywhere else I can think to look. If there's a clue here, it's either invisible or it was stolen by the jerk who broke in here last week."

"We don't know that." Logan sat down across from her, his face serious. "We can't give up, Rory. Your dad found something on Reaper's Point. I'm guessing it's the killer's hiding place, his body dump. It's something the killer was willing to protect. If your old man was running true to form, he documented it."

A surge of gumption pulsed through her. "You're right." She leaned forward on the couch.

Think, Rory...think. She stood up, pacing in front of the picture window, staring across the draw.

"Do you suppose the killer was watching my father?" The thought gave her pause. She turned to stare at Logan. "That would explain why he felt compelled to hide the femur bone, rather than leaving it in plain sight. It would stand to reason, he'd have hidden anything else he'd thought the killer might discover before he could expose him."

Logan came to his feet. "If he was being watched and he'd known it, he'd have used a hiding place that blended in with his routine. Something the killer wouldn't suspect."

"Someplace that fit. Someplace where the act of hiding wouldn't raise suspicion." Rory strode into the kitchen. It had been her father's favorite room in the house. A place where he'd experimented with food concoctions, some fantastic, some inedible.

Her gaze settled on the refrigerator. He'd been the king of burritos. Anything you could put in a flour shell was his idea of a meal.

Pulling open the door, she stared at the only packet of burrito shells in the frig. It would be the perfect hiding place. A place the killer could easily overlook.

Reaching in, she pulled the package out of the refrigerator and opened it, dumping the shells out onto the counter.

"I don't believe it," she whispered.

Visible between the stack of tortilla shells was the corner of a sheet of paper. Excitement churned her insides, as she shuffled the paper out from between the shells.

"This is it. This is what he was hiding."

Logan moved up beside her as she studied the drawing, trying to decipher what it was and how it fit in.

A series of lines streamed down the page from a single point.

"These could be drainages off of the mountain. It looks a lot like the paper we found in his backpack."

"Could be. There are seven of them," Logan said.

One of the lines was crossed with an *X* and the letters *RL* next to it. "This could be Reaper's Ledge." Running her finger over to the next line with an *X* on it, she mentally made the trip.

"This is Bailey's Draw, on the other side of the north face. There are tons of caves and hollows there. Most of them have been boarded up to prevent accidents. You could disappear in one of those and never come out."

They'd set up camp a quarter of a mile from the area that night, five years ago. She'd been found in the ravine below the trail leading into the Bailey Creek drainage.

Logan's hand on her back made her jump. Her heart pounded in her chest as she mentally challenged the fear that threatened to take over logical thought. She couldn't let it happen. Not now. Not when they finally had a chance to nail the bastard who'd nearly killed her.

"Take a breath, Rory." Logan stroked her back.

She closed her eyes, taking in the safety of his touch.

"I'm not going to let anything happen to you. We'll get this maniac."

Logan pulled her into his arms, pressing her against him with an intensity that mirrored the concern racing in his blood. Dr. Matson had provided them with the best clue he'd had in years. X marks the spot. The spot where he'd discovered the bones. Maybe even the spot where the killer had taken Rory that night. Where he'd done unspeakable things to her.

Anger ground through him. It was time to bring him in. Time to rain down unrelenting justice on the man who'd hurt her. He only hoped he'd know when to stop, before he killed the SOB with his bare hands.

Logan held her for what seemed an eternity, but it wasn't long enough. He stared out of the plate-glass window from over the top of her head, trying to put the puzzle together.

The trees on the other side of the gulch, two-hundred yards away, were dense. Their canopy had grown together in a lush mass of deep green. It was a perfect place to hide. A place to watch.

Excitement coursed through him as he released Rory and stepped toward the window. "Feel like a hike?"

She moved up next to him. "Yeah."

"That's the only vantage point that would give him a view into this place. He'd have a pinpoint shot right through these windows."

"Privacy wasn't a concern for my dad. He didn't even want blinds on these windows. It spoiled the scenery. The killer could have monitored everything he did in these two rooms. Come on." Logan took her hand as they left the cabin through the door that led out onto the deck.

The air was still and cold. Not a breeze. Not a sound. There was a storm coming. Snow.

A shiver raked Rory's skin as they weaved their way down the narrow trail into the ravine where a shallow stream babbled over river rock in a never-ending attempt to get off the mountain.

She needed that, too. But she also needed to know who'd been watching her father. Who'd wanted his discovery to die with him.

She paused at the edge of the creek.

In one fell swoop, Logan picked her up and stepped into the knee-deep water. Sloshing across to the other side he set her on her feet. "Wouldn't want you to get wet."

She grinned up at him, taken with his sheepish grin. "My hero with a melted cast."

"Bah! It's fiberglass. Indestructible."

His smile faded and her heart squeezed.

"Logan… I want you to know, I don't blame you anymore. You weren't responsible for the things that happened that night."

He raised his hand to her face, cupping her cheek. His eyes narrowed. "Tell that to my heart. Because I almost died right along with you. It about killed your old man, too. He ranted around like a man obsessed, until he started to comb this mountain for some relief. Both of us would have done anything to help you that night…even given our lives in the fight, if it would have saved you even one second of pain…."

Rory's heart jolted in her chest as she studied his face. Rugged, but handsome. Square jawline and deep brown eyes that could melt her doubts like butter in the sun. It was the face of the man she loved beyond reason and she knew at that very moment he would have died for her that night if she'd have asked him to.

"I could never live with that kind of sacrifice. Let's just get him this time."

"That's my girl. Come on."

Bolting forward they picked up a narrow game trail as it pushed deep into the trees. Slowly, they moved through the forest, each step measured as they studied everything around them.

"Look at that," Logan said, pointing up into the trees.

Rory stopped behind him, following the line of his finger.

"What is it?" She stared at the contraption locked in between two pines, standing several feet apart.

"Haven't you ever seen a tree stand?"

"I think so." She studied the structure of metal bars, fitted with a wooden deck. "They're for hunting, aren't they?"

"Yeah. You can sit up there undetected and watch the game walk by. But I'd bet our hunter wasn't after elk or bear."

He reached for a low branch and pulled himself up.

"Be careful. You're my bridge over the river."

Logan smiled down at her and resumed his assent until he reached the tree stand and stepped onto the platform.

Straightening, he turned toward the other side of the ravine.

The branches had been trimmed back, leaving a clear view of the cabin directly across the draw. A view that would have afforded the killer intimate knowledge of Dr. Matson's movements.

Logan sobered, glancing down to where Rory moved around the tree trunks. "What are you looking for?"

"This." She squatted next to a print in the dirt.

Logan's mouth went dry, the confirmation putting a knot in his gut. He'd recognize the killer's boot track anywhere. This was his eye on the world. He'd probably been watching Rory from the time she arrived back in Reaper's Point.

He swallowed, thankful he'd convinced her to stay at the condo. "I need a picture and we'll get out of here." Logan climbed down and took a photo of the familiar print. He snagged Rory's hand as they made their way back toward the cabin. He had an interrogation date. He didn't want to keep Brady Morris waiting any longer.

"WHERE WERE YOU last Saturday night around midnight?"

"Sleeping, I guess." Morris glared at him. "And what if I don't want to answer any more of your questions before my lawyer gets here."

"Then, I guess, I'm out of luck, but I'll still have my search warrant."

"Why the hell would you need a search warrant, Brewer?"

"Because, your alibi sucks. And because it sucks, I plan to take your place apart a piece at a time until I find what I'm looking for."

"What's this really about?" Morris asked, a defiant glare in his eyes.

"What were you doing on Reaper's Point Monday morning. You can't deny you were there. I saw you myself."

"I was hiking. It was my day off. That's not a crime."

"It is if you intentionally pushed my deputy off the jump point."

"Now, wait a minute. I never shoved anyone off the point and I sure as hell didn't see your deputy up there."

Logan let out a breath and stood up. He'd hit a wall with Morris. The guy was either a good liar or not their guy.

"When was the last time you spoke to Gale Robins?"

Brady's face went pale.

Logan pushed forward. "We found her remains and you were the last one to see her alive."

"Bullshit. She was alive and kicking when I drove her to the bus station in Cliff Side. She was headed back to L.A."

"She never made it."

"That's it. I'm not saying another word until my lawyer gets here."

"Then, you won't mind remaining silent in a jail cell. I'm going to hold you, Morris. You can't or won't account for your whereabouts. I don't know if it's ego or stupidity, but we'll see what the search turns up."

Morris sat stone-faced as Logan left the interrogation room.

Frustration circulated in his veins.

Sparks came in the front door of the station, waving a warrant in his hand. "We got it. Judge McNair."

"Great. Let's go. I'll get Rory." Logan looked up to where Rory sat in his office, staring back at him through the glass.

A slow smile turned her mouth as she stood up and came around the desk.

There was tension in the air. It had been building since they'd discovered the tree stand and the boot print, but it would be over soon.

"Ready?" he asked, feeling her hesitation.

"I'd rather stay here. It's police business. I don't want to muddy the waters."

"Are you afraid of what we'll find?"

Her downcast gaze gave away her true feelings, but she quickly looked up at him. "Damn right. If Morris is the one, his place will be loaded with trinkets and trophies. My abductor took the necklace my mother gave me the year before she died."

"I remember. Your Black Hills gold cross."

"I'd like it back, but I don't want to go fishing for it. It'll be better if I stay here."

"Better for you, but not for me. You have to ride along, Aurora. You can sit in the car, but I'm not letting you out of my protection. Not this late in the game."

He watched her swallow and squared his shoulders, preparing for a fight. He couldn't explain why, but caution still hissed along his nerve endings. Even though they had Morris in lock up, he wanted to be sure they had their man before he left her alone.

"I'll get my jacket." Her shoulders slumped with resignation as she slipped back into the office and pulled it off the back of his chair.

"Just hang with me. This search won't take long." He held open the door for her and followed her outside to the patrol car. It was a temporary ride while the Blazer was in the shop for body work and a severed brake line.

Logan opened the back door and she got inside. He moved around to the passenger side and climbed in next to Sparks. "Let's go."

Rory sat quietly in the backseat, staring through the metal mesh barrier that separated the seats. It was an odd feeling being closed inside the car. Glancing around she noticed there were no inside door handles.

"That's how I keep the bad ones in," Sparks said.

She glanced up, catching his gaze in the rear-view mirror. She should laugh at his obvious joke, but a chill grazed her skin as she stared back into his eyes, before looking away.

"Back off, Deputy. She's my prisoner."

The sound of Logan's humorous summation calmed her nerves. She was his, but she'd come willingly and she planned to stay willingly if he asked her to.

"No problem. You're the boss," Sparks said.

Rory watched the scenery flit past the window as they turned toward the lake, now void of boat traffic. With the dying of the summer heat and the crisp feel of fall in the air, the lakefront turned still when the summer people left. It almost seemed like the water sighed, too, at peace and ready to embrace winter.

Sparks pulled into a short drive and parked next to a small cottage. "This is it."

"Nice place," she said from behind the barrier. She suddenly wanted to go inside. Wanted to rummage around hoping to find a piece from her past. A measure of closure that had eluded her all of these years, but she wouldn't dare risk a solid case against Morris. That need far outweighed her desire to find the necklace inside the cottage. So she'd wait in the car.

"Sit tight." Logan climbed out of the car.

She watched him and Sparks step up onto the deck, realizing she was a prisoner in the car until they returned. Maybe it was better that way. She wouldn't be tempted to snoop around.

The sound of tires on gravel drew her attention as a sleek black car pulled in next to the police unit.

A man climbed out.

One look at his slick suit told her he was a lawyer, Brady Morris' lawyer, and he was here to assess the search.

She slumped back into the seat and sucked in a breath. He had no way of stopping it. If they were going to find anything on Morris, they could still do it with a lawyer looking over their shoulder.

He stepped up onto the deck and entered the cottage.

An hour later, he emerged with Sparks and Logan behind him.

Rory leaned forward in the seat, staring at the men as they talked outside of the house.

Her stomach lurched. Her gaze locked on Logan's gloved hand. Pinched between his thumb and index finger were a pair of boots.

A pair of Sierra Madre hiking boots.

Clawing where there should have been a handle, she fought to get out of the car, but couldn't.

She banged on the window, drawing Logan's attention. He slid the boots into a large paper bag that Sparks held open and turned in her direction.

"Let me out," she mouthed to him as he approached the door and popped the latch.

Near panic took a hold of her as she climbed out of the car and tried to compose herself.

The lawyer moved past her and climbed into his car.

"Did you get anything?" she asked, her heart pounding in her chest.

"Yeah. We found a pair of hiking boots, but then, you knew that."

She shook her head. "I saw you put them in the bag. Are they the ones?" She stared up at him, hope churning her insides.

"It looks like it, Rory. They're the same brand, but the only way to be sure is a side-by-side comparison."

Her knees threatened to buckle as she leaned into him. A surge of relief coursed through her veins and warmed her cheeks. "Anything else? Did you find anything else?"

"Nothing. Just the boots in the back of his closet."

Disappointment twisted up her spine as she pulled back.

The boots were significant. They were the only piece of solid identifying evidence they'd ever had in the case. Matching them to Morris was huge. So why didn't she feel better. Why hadn't certainty spread to every corner of her mind?

"We'll get them back to the evidence room and make a casting." Logan pulled open the door for her and she slipped into the prison on wheels, determined to take some comfort in the find.

"THEY'RE NOT A MATCH," Sparks said, stepping back from the two tread castings laying side by side on the counter.

Logan pulled in a breath and crossed his arms over his chest. He'd been so damned sure they'd finally caught the killer, he'd put so much hope in this single piece of evidence.

Taking another close look for comparison, he let reality sink in. Rory had mentioned there should be trophies in Morris's house. Items he'd taken from his victims. But they'd only found the boots. Boots Morris claimed he'd gotten from his father as a

Christmas gift seven years ago and never worn. The tread wear-pattern confirmed it.

In addition, one of his buddies had come forward, probably on the advice of the lawyer, and claimed Brady had been at the bar with him on Saturday night until closing.

"Cut Morris loose."

Logan's gut tightened. He was not only in evidentiary oblivion, he was tanked in the bottom of a black hole with no way out.

Rory sat quietly in Logan's office, fighting the dread that flowed through her veins like a numbing poison.

Brady Morris had strutted out of the station a free man, but not before pausing at the office window to smile at her for an instant. A slow, catch-me-if-you-can smile that chilled her to the bone.

Chapter Eleven

Logan held Rory in his arms, letting the slow rhythm of the song move them as one.

The annual Harvest Ball was a Reaper's Point tradition. A chance for everyone in town to come together and enjoy live music, food and each other's company before the long winter hibernation began.

The song ended and the band rocked it up with a loud rendition of "Sweet Home Alabama."

Logan took Rory's hand, leading her off the dance floor in the middle of the town square to a park bench on the fringes of the grass.

"It feels good to do something normal," she said, sitting down next to him. Tipping her head back, she gazed at the night sky. "Look at the stars."

Logan leaned back, too, staring at the pristine glow of billions of gaseous balls of fire. "Beautiful."

"I miss seeing them. The lights of the city drown them out. I'd forgotten how gorgeous they are."

He hesitated as he glanced over at her. He wanted her to stay in Reaper's Point.

"There's something I need to ask you."

"Okay." She looked at him and his nerve melted. He was six years too late and a captured and convicted killer shy of resolution.

She must have sensed his dilemma, because she took his hand and pulled him to his feet. "Come on. Let's walk home. I'm tired."

Logan fell in step with her, moving down the sidewalk of festivalgoers, feeling like a fool.

"Look, Rory. I'm not very good at this, but you know how I feel about you."

She stopped in her tracks, staring across the street.

"What is it?" He followed her line of sight, but didn't see anything out of the ordinary.

"It's him. The man I saw on the mountain the day we found victim number seven."

"What are you talking about?"

"He's the guy with the gray beard and the ball cap."

Logan spotted the man, moving down the middle of the street in a staggering stride. His heart rate revved as he stared at the man's boots.

"Come on. We've got to follow him." He took Rory's hand, steering her into the street. Casually, they dodged other people, hanging back behind the man who'd picked up his pace and glanced over his shoulder several times.

"Tell me again when you saw him."

"The day you broke your leg. I was following the team off the mountain, but you got ahead of me. In the first tree grove, I ran into him. He struck me as being out of place."

"He's out of place, all right. Take a look at his boots."

Rory's stomach squeezed. She wanted to turn tail and run, but Logan's pull was too great.

"They look like Sierra Madre. They go for 500 bucks. They're the same brand the killer wears."

"You got it, sweetheart."

"He doesn't look like he can afford a coat, how can he be wearing expensive boots?"

"I don't know. But I'm going to find out. I'm going to detain him for questioning, but there's no way I can catch him with this leg if he spots us and takes off."

"Should we call for backup?"

"Yeah, but I don't want him to spot me with my handheld radio. It'll tip him off. He could bolt."

Rory spotted a phone booth up ahead on the corner of Main and Second. "I'm going to stop at the pay phone and call 9-1-1. You keep following him and I'll catch up with you before you get to Fourth Street."

Logan glanced over at her. She could read the worry in his eyes.

"Hey. There are people everywhere and I can scream like a banshee. We can't let him get away."

"You're right. Let's do it."

Caution stirred in her blood as they moved closer to the phone. He didn't seem like the killer type, but what was the killer type? She believed anyone could kill if their motivation was strong enough.

Logan let go of her hand next to the phone and continued his jaunt down the street, never missing a step.

Her hands shook as she picked up the receiver and dialed 9-1-1.

"Belle County 9-1-1. What's your emergency?"

"I'm calling in for Sheriff Brewer. He's in pursuit of a man for questioning and he needs a backup officer to intercept."

"What's his location?"

"He's on Main Street, between Second and Fourth."

"I'll dispatch Deputy Taylor. He's in close proximity to Brewer's location."

"Thank you."

"You're welcome."

Rory hung up the phone and took off at a fast walk, catching up with Logan about the time Deputy Taylor turned onto Main Street from Fourth.

The man stopped the instant he saw the police car make the corner and veered down the alley connecting Main and Pleasant.

"He's running!" Logan shouted to Deputy Taylor as he stopped and jumped out of his patrol car.

"The alley. Get some more backup. We can't lose him."

Taylor talked into the two-way radio attached to his collar and took off down the alley at a dead run.

"Get in!" Logan shouted. "We'll cut him off on the other side."

Rory obeyed, climbing into the cop car.

Logan flipped on the lights, put it in gear, stepped on the gas and turned around in the street.

Maneuvering, he raced up the block and took Fourth Street over in time to see Deputy Taylor coming out of the alley escorting the man.

Logan stopped the car and climbed out.

Rory followed.

"Good job. Take him to the station, I'll be there within the hour."

"What's this about?" the man asked, clearly intoxicated.

"Those boots. Where'd you get them?"

"I know my rights," he slurred. "I don't have to say a thing and you can pay for my damn lawyer, too."

"Get him out of here," Logan said, watching Taylor put the man in the backseat of the patrol car. "And confiscate his boots the minute you get him into the station. They're evidence."

Rory tried to relax. She'd been face to face with the man. Maybe he really had been watching her that day in the woods. Gooseflesh raised on her arms, even though she was wearing a bulky sweater.

"And can you send a patrol car around to pick us up?"

"Sure thing."

She watched the patrol car pull away and stared at Logan then down at his exposed cast. "You're destroying that thing. Look at this crack." She ran her finger along a six-inch split in the fiberglass.

"It's nothing some duct tape can't fix."

"Yeah, right." She smiled up at him, taking his hand. "Let's sit and wait for the car. You can't be on that leg anymore tonight."

"Okay, doc. What'll we do in the meantime? Neck?"

"That sounds wonderful."

He pulled her into his arms in the middle of the street and kissed her until her blood came to a boil.

LOGAN LAY AWAKE long after midnight, his mind working the details of the case. Rory lay next to him, curled in the crook of his arm.

Something wasn't right. A recurring loop of information kept spinning in his brain, begging to be analyzed.

The boots the transient, James Milo, had been wearing were a perfect match to the tread casting from Rory's case and from outside the cabin. But the man had been too drunk to deliver a coherent sentence, much less implicate himself in the crimes. Logan planned to question Milo in the morning after he'd had time to sleep it off.

Tucking his head, he buried his face in Rory's hair and breathed in her scent, an intoxicating mix of sweet vanilla and musk. Making love to her was as fantastic as it had ever been, maybe better.

He planned to ask her to stay. Forever, if she'd have him. Convicting her abductor would go a long way to keeping her in Reaper's Point. If only the facts would support a conviction.

A gust of wind rattled the storm shutters outside the window, setting his nerves on edge. The radio had predicted the first big storm of the fall season. It was due to hit midmorning.

His officers had spent the late afternoon getting the word out to the hikers and climbers considering a trek up the mountain, but he worried about the ones they'd been unable to warn in time.

He pulled Rory closer, enjoying the heat coming from her naked body. He instantly wanted her with a hunger that never seemed to leave his system.

The police radio on the bedside table startled him, the gravely hiss of the transmission setting his nerves on edge.

Logan separated himself from her, sat up and turned on the lamp, listening for the details of the dispatch.

"Belle County Sheriff, Belle County dispatch, please respond."

He snagged the portable radio from its charger base and pressed the talk button. "This is Brewer. What's the trouble?"

"A caller on 9-1-1 reports picking up a man at

4:00 a.m. near the bottom of Reaper's Point. He's being transported to the police station. The man claims someone took his wife from their tent."

A cold chill streaked down Logan's spine and froze into a knot in his stomach.

Rory bolted upright next to him.

"Copy, dispatch. I'll be en route to the station in ten minutes. I want every officer called in. Page the Search-and-Rescue team, contact the state troopers in Cliff Side and have the search chopper warming up on the pad."

"Copy that. Belle County dispatch. Clear."

"Zero-five-eight-seven-three clear."

Logan laid the radio down on the nightstand and stood up.

It was happening again. Fighting the dread that rushed in his veins, he got dressed. He had to keep it together. Had to move carefully or another young woman would die.

"I'm coming with you." Rory climbed out of bed and disappeared into the bathroom, returning a short time later, dressed and ready to go.

He watched her open the bedside table and pull out her belt, holster and gun. She methodically put it on. He could see her hands shake as she straightened and leveled her gaze on him.

"The M.O. matches my abduction."

"Looks that way, sweetheart. I'd hoped to hell we had him under lock and key."

In two steps, she was in his arms. He pulled her

close, breathed her in. "We'll get him this time. I'm tapping everything we've got."

"Thank God. I just hope it's in time to save her." Rory took his hand and they left the condo, headed for the station.

Dawn was breaking over Reaper's Point, highlighting the gathering of thick black storm clouds.

"Let's hope those are packing rain." She nodded toward the mountain.

"Snow could hold up a search." Logan climbed into his pickup and Rory slid into the passenger seat.

"We'll take it by air. Are you up for it?"

She glanced over at him. "Yes."

"We'll do an aerial search of the ravine on your father's drawing."

Concern twisted around her nerves. What if they'd misinterpreted the map? What if they lost valuable time, following a bunch of meaningless lines leading to nowhere?

Frustration pooled in her veins. She fought to still the myriad of conflicting thoughts bubbling in her brain. They would do the best they could with the information they had.

"That's as good as it gets. We can beat the search teams up the mountain by at least an hour."

Logan backed out of the driveway and headed for the station where teams were already gathering in the gloomy predawn light. This was the calm before the storm. He could feel it in his bones. Their search window would close in less than three hours. Tension bound itself to the muscles between his shoulder blades as they hustled into the station.

The place was abuzz with activity. His officers were busy shoving gear into backpacks and lacing up their boots.

"Where's Sparks?"

Deputy Taylor looked up from his desk. "Called in sick this morning. Says he ate something bad last night at the festival and can't leave the powder room. He's going to try to make it in by ten or so."

"Let's hope he takes the pink stuff. We're going to be shorthanded without him. Where's the witness?"

"Mr. Rapaport is in your office. We got him a blanket and a cup of hot coffee. He was half frozen by the time he got here."

Sympathy clamped onto Logan's insides as he studied the back of the man sitting in the chair in front of his desk.

He glanced around and saw Rory disappear into the break room.

"This call came in late last night for Ms. Matson." Deputy Taylor held out a Post-it.

"I'll give it to her later." Logan snagged the note, shoved it into his shirt pocket and turned toward his office.

He stepped inside and closed the door.

The man instantly sat forward and turned slightly.

"Mr. Rapaport. I'm Sheriff Brewer." Logan proceeded around his desk and sat down, studying the man dressed in jeans and a T-shirt. His guess put the man's age at around twenty-five.

"You have to find her." A note of desperation accentuated the tremor in his voice.

"We're going to do everything we can. Search and Rescue is about to take off. I've got a chopper on the pad. We'll find her." He stopped before the words *I promise* left his lips.

This was a promise he wasn't sure he could keep. It was déjà vu for him. He'd sat in Mr. Rapaport's chair. Felt his terror, rage and frustration.

"Can you tell me exactly what happened when you noticed your wife missing? I also need a physical description of her for my report."

"The wind woke me up. That's when I saw the hole in the back of the tent. It was flapping in the breeze. I got my flashlight and when I shined it in her direction…her sleeping bag was empty. I yelled for her…but she didn't answer. That's when I headed off the mountain."

"Can you describe her and what she was wearing?"

"She's five foot six, a hundred-and-forty pounds. Brown hair, blue eyes. Flannel pajamas. Yellow, I think. Her name is Mary." The man's eyes went watery, his words catching in his throat. "For God's sake, she doesn't have her shoes."

Logan's heart sagged in his chest. His throat

tightened. The comparison was almost identical to Rory's on that night six years ago. His gut twisted.

"Stay here. Try to relax. We'll let you know the minute we find anything."

"Thank you." Mr. Rapaport's head dropped forward into his hands.

Logan left the office. He wanted to explode, here, now, but he needed to channel his energy in a constructive manner. Finding Mary Rapaport before the killer did what he did best.

He swallowed the lump in his throat and glanced up as Rory came out of the break room with a cup of coffee in hand.

"Are you ready? I've got a chopper waiting on the pad just outside of town. We can be over Reaper's Point in fifteen minutes."

"Let's go."

Deputy Taylor stood up, carried over a piece of paper and handed it to Logan.

"Here's the grid map Search and Rescue is using. Mr. Rapaport said they were camped half a mile or so above the Base-Camp parking lot."

Logan studied the map, working scenarios out in his mind. It was unlikely the killer would stay close to the camp, but there were plenty of places to hide. It was close to where they'd found victim number seven.

"Have them work their way out from the campsite. We'll join the search from the air in approximately an hour."

"You got it." Taylor turned to find the team leader.

"Hey, Taylor."

"Yeah?"

"Did the old man have an explanation for where he got those five-hundred-dollar hiking boots?"

"Yes. Hell of a thing. He claims he found them in the Dumpster out behind the grocery store two days ago."

"Cut him loose. He's not our guy. Make sure he gets a hot breakfast this morning and the number for Social Services."

"Okay." Deputy Taylor turned away, disappearing into the back of the station where they locked up prisoners.

Rory slipped on her backpack and joined Logan at the front door. They moved outside, where the air had taken on a cool nip that cut through the layers of clothing he wore—right down to his bulletproof vest.

A formidable bank of clouds had descended, encasing the tip of Reaper's Point in a sheath of darkness.

Logan pulled his collar up, but it was no defense against the chill in his bones or the foreboding that pressed on his nerves like a vise.

Time was running out.

Chapter Twelve

The high-pitched whir of the rotor blades hummed in Rory's ears and set her teeth on edge. She'd never been hot on flying; she liked the feel of the earth under her feet.

"We're clear for takeoff." The pilot, Dick Murdock, said into the headset Rory wore.

"Where do you want to go, Sheriff?"

"The north face and down into the Bailey Creek drainage. We'll rendezvous a half mile east of the Base-Camp parking lot in one hour so we can shadow the rescue teams."

"Copy that." The pilot pulled back on the stick and applied the throttle.

Rory's stomach lurched as the Bell Textron 407 lifted off the pad and accelerated forward, picking up altitude as they streaked toward the mountain.

Logan turned in his seat next to the pilot, handing Rory a pair of binoculars.

"Use these. Look for anything moving on the

ground." He hesitated. "If it helps, her name is Mary Rapaport."

She nodded and took the field glasses, determined to scan every inch of the terrain below. A woman's life depended on catching a glimpse of her location amongst the dense trees and undergrowth.

Knowing her name made it personal.

Doubt coiled inside of her. If only she hadn't been blindfolded when the killer dragged her into his lair. If only she'd been able to see something, anything.

Rory raised the binoculars to her eyes and adjusted the focus, pulling in a clear image of the ground four-hundred-feet below.

The pilot turned the chopper parallel to the mountain, giving them a clear view.

Through the glasses, she spotted the jump-off point for the north face. "The jump point is clear."

"Affirmative." Logan's voice sounded inside her headset, making her heart beat a little faster. Did he know how she felt about him? Did he have any idea how much she needed him?

"Want to attack Bailey Creek next?" the pilot asked.

"Yeah. Stay to the south. Up where the caves are."

"Copy that."

Rory felt the *g*-force suck her to the seat of the chopper as they took a hard left.

Raising the binoculars, she focused on the cliff face as they rounded the crest of the mountain.

A light-colored flash caught her attention against the chunk of granite filling the lens.

"Hold up. Can you hover?"

"Sure." The pilot flailed the rotors.

"I thought I saw something on the cliff face." Roaming the granite with the binoculars, she settled on Reaper's Ledge and cleared the sight picture with the focus button.

Her breath caught in her lungs.

Horror washing over her mind in one crushing wave as the image imprinted on her brain.

"Do you see her, Logan?"

"Yes."

Fear squeezed her insides as she stared into the field glasses.

Mary Rapaport lay on Reaper's Ledge, a prisoner on the three-by-seven-foot sickle of granite. If she could only reach through the glasses, she was sure she could touch her, help her.

Rory methodically studied the scene, knowing it was the killer's handiwork. Mary was blindfolded. Her hands tied in front of her…but she was moving.

"She's alive, Logan! I saw her move." Excitement seized her, but the realization was quickly overshadowed as she watched Mary struggle against her bonds, moving closer and closer to the edge.

"Has this bird got a PA?" Logan asked.

"Yeah," the pilot said.

"We've got to stop her from rolling off the ledge."

Rory tried to relax as she watched Mary Rapaport, naked and bound, move to within feet of sudden death.

"Mary Rapaport. This is Sheriff Logan Brewer. Stop moving. Lay perfectly still. You're on a ledge. Search and Rescue is on the way. Hang on."

The sound of Logan's voice stilled the woman.

Rory lowered the binoculars, allowing an instant of relief to flood her system. Mary was going to make it.

"Cliff Side Tower. This is Rescue Ten." The pilot's voice echoed in the headphone. "The victim has been located. She's in need of rescue and medical assistance. Location is Reaper's Ledge on the north face of Reaper's Point."

"Copy that, Rescue Ten, I'll advise Belle County dispatch. They can relay to their teams on the ground. Cliff Side Tower, clear."

Logan closed his eyes for a second, letting the information penetrate his brain. Mary Rapaport was alive. But he couldn't get his head around the circumstances. Why was she breathing when none of his other victims were, with the exception of Rory?

Rory.

"Get us out of here, Murdock. She's bait!" Panic

locked onto Logan's nerves the moment he spotted the red dot on Dick Murdock's chest, but it was too late.

The hollow sound of metal ripping through plastic raked over his eardrums.

He stared in horror as the pilot jolted in the seat next to him, grabbing for his chest. Bright red blood spread across the front of his shirt.

Another blast ripped into the cockpit, catching Logan in the chest, he rocked forward as the repercussion shook him, but the bullet lodged in his vest.

Dick yanked the stick, pulling it hard to the left.

The chopper veered off.

"Have you got it?" Logan yelled into the headset microphone.

"Down...I'll put it down." Clutching his chest, Dick Murdock aimed for the ground at the base of the north face.

Logan reached into the backseat and grabbed Rory's hand. "We're going in. Hang on."

"Brace! We're going down hard," the pilot warned.

Logan squeezed Rory's hand, praying they'd live as he watched the ground come up like a rocket.

The thud was deafening. The impact violent.

The cockpit collapsed around them like chalk on granite and listed hard to the left.

The whine of the chopper's rotor blades sliced into his consciousness, warning him the worse was yet to come.

One by one the four blades gnashed into the ground.

The strikes sent bone-jarring vibrations rattling through the remains of the chopper, tearing it apart.

Logan popped his seat belt.

He reached over to assist Dick Murdock, but it was too late.

Regret hissed through him as he checked for a pulse. Nothing.

The air around them was permeated with the smell of jet fuel. A tank must have ruptured.

Panic rocked his nerves as he pulled the door handle, but it wouldn't budge.

"Come on, Rory. We've got to get out of here."

Turning, Logan rammed his boot against the door.

It popped open.

Rory unfastened her seat belt, grabbed her pack and climbed over the seat.

Together they crawled out of the aircraft on the high side.

The rotor blades were still spinning, hacking into the ground on the left side of the aircraft.

"Stay low," Logan demanded. One wrong move and they'd be chopped to bits.

On their bellies, they crawled until they cleared the end of the blades.

Coming to his knees, Logan stood up. "We've got to get away from the wreck." They bolted for a rock outcropping and crawled behind it.

Logan pulled Rory into his arms and closed his eyes. They were safe for the moment, but the killer had planned this and he'd used Mary Rapaport to get them into position.

He couldn't let his guard down for one second as long as they were all on the mountain together.

"The chopper is going to go. I smelled jet fuel. All it needs is a spark."

She tensed in his arms.

"We're safe behind these rocks. Rescue is on the way, the radio message went out before Murdock was shot. They'll get to Mary."

"Shot…you mean someone killed him?"

"To bring the helicopter down."

"He'll never stop. Not until he finishes what he started." A sob shook her body and Logan pulled her closer.

"We're going to make it. We're both armed."

From the wreckage, he heard a pop, then another.

Bracing for the explosion, he covered Rory's head with his hands.

In a violent burst of fuel and flames, the fuselage blew apart sending debris raining down around them. The heat was intense. Only the rock barrier protected them from the explosion.

"You've been shot." Rory's voice was a whisper against his neck.

He looked down to where she toyed with the hole in his uniform just below his heart. "Good thing it's a cold day. I like the extra heat I can generate inside my vest and it does wonders at stopping bullets, but I also lost my radio in the crash. We have no communication."

She gazed up at him, her face paling before his eyes.

"We've got to get out of here, Rory."

"What about the rescuers? We have to wait for them. We can't leave this location. How will they find us?"

"There's no time. He shot the pilot to bring the chopper down. He's desperate and willing to do whatever it takes to get to you."

Her mouth opened, but no sound came out.

Logan scanned the tree line a hundred feet below their position. The shot could have come from there. Hell, it could have come from anywhere. They were stationary targets. They had to take cover in the trees.

"Are you all right?"

"I think so."

"We're going to head straight down the mountain. Stay low." He took her hand as they came to their feet. "Go."

Logan picked a line and focused on it. Determined to get to safety. He suspected the killer had missed his kill shot when Murdock rocked the helicopter to the left. He wouldn't miss again.

The loose rock gave under his feet as he pulled Rory down the mountainside at a hobbling run.

Shards of granite cartwheeled past them, but he kept moving until he reached the trees and ducked in behind the trunk of a massive Tamarack.

Working to catch his breath, he felt searing pain when he inhaled. The killer's bullet striking his vest may have broken some of his ribs.

Rory leaned against the tree, staring into the dense forest like a leery rabbit bent on detecting the wolf.

He didn't blame her, there were wolves out here and probably closer than he could guess.

"Are you okay?"

"Yeah." She stared up at him.

"We've got to keep moving."

She nodded. "If we travel south, we'll eventually reach the Base-Camp parking lot."

He considered her suggestion. It made sense, but it would be too obvious. The killer was probably waiting to the south, assuming they'd run straight for the rescue teams launching from Base-Camp.

"We're going to go north and drop off the lower ridge onto the southeast end of the lake."

"But that's too far away. The other way is shorter and there's help there."

"There's also a killer who took a shot at us with a laser-sighted rifle. That puts him smack in the middle between us and help."

Rory flinched. "You're right. That's the path of least resistance and he's probably on it."

"Come on, let's stick to the trees and keep moving, he won't stay patient for long. And tread lightly, we don't want to give him an easy trail to follow."

Logan moved forward, careful to step where ground cover displaced his tracks. Working down the mountainside, they reached the bottom of the draw twenty minutes later.

Exhaustion cramped his muscles.

The air around them had grown colder in the time it took to hike to the bottom.

He stopped for a breather and sat down on a boulder.

Rory sat down next to him.

"It's going to snow. I can feel it." She blew a puff of breath into the air, watching it turn frosty white.

"The temperature has dropped ten degrees since we crashed. We need to find shelter. Hole up somewhere if it starts to snow." Logan gazed back up at the north face high above them, now barely visible through the trees.

If the weather went bad, there would be no search for them until it cleared. The prospect of spending the night on the mountain left him with a bad feeling in the pit of his stomach. But if that was what it took to keep Rory safe, he'd spend a hundred nights up here.

A faint mechanical beep caught Logan's attention. He tried to judge it's location. "What was that?"

Rory's expression brightened. "My walkie-talkie! I forgot all about it. I always carry it in my backpack. My dad made me keep it for emergencies. This qualifies."

An instant of relief surged in his veins. Communications could save their lives. If the radio had any range, they could contact the rescue team with their exact location.

Rory frantically dug into her backpack, finally finding the single walkie-talkie at the bottom. "I forgot to get the mate back from Sparks after his launch off of the ledge. Thank God."

She pushed the talk button. "Hello. Can you hear me? Hello. Do you copy?"

The airwaves crackled to life, making her heart jump in her chest.

"Copy. This is Wade Sparks, is that you, Rory?"

Excitement shot through her. They were going to be okay. Sparks would send help, all they had to do was wait. "Yes. The chopper crashed, but Logan and I made it out alive."

"Copy that. I'm just leaving Base-Camp lot. What's your twenty?"

"We're approximately half a mile north of the north face at the bottom of the draw."

Silence greeted her last transmission. Frustrated, she shook the radio. "Please don't die. I should have recharged the batteries…."

"Copy that. I'll relay the information to Search and Rescue. Hang on. Help's on the way."

Relief spread over her as she stared up at Logan. "We're safe. Help's coming." She closed her eyes and rolled her head from side to side in an attempt to release some of the stress in her neck. The impact of the crash had probably left her battered and bruised in places she didn't even know about. But tomorrow would bring it home.

She opened her eyes and reached for Logan's hand. "I need you," she whispered as she lay her cheek against his shoulder.

Logan sucked in a breath and tried to relax, but the tension in the air was palpable. Help was on the way, but there was still a killer on the mountain who had to be dealt with.

Without warning, the sky overhead opened up. Bone chilling rain pelted down on them like BBs.

Logan stared, searching for shelter. Their best bet was going back up into the tree line. They had to try and stay dry. The first rule of survival.

"Come on. Let's run for it."

Rory glanced up at him. Her face blanched, her mouth opened.

Thud.

Pain burned across the back of his head, turning everything black for an instant. He reached for the gun in his holster.

Thud.

Another blow cracked against his skull, but this time the darkness didn't retreat.

It swallowed him whole.

Chapter Thirteen

Awareness knifed into Logan, sending shards of pain stabbing into his brain.

Hard rain pounded on his face. A shiver racked his body, followed by another and another in unrelenting succession.

He attempted to open his eyes, but only one responded. Staring up at the dark clouds overhead, he tried to put together the disjointed string of thoughts circling in his mind.

He was on Reaper's Point.

Rolling onto his belly, he dragged himself to a rock, using it to pull himself to his feet, he leaned against it to keep from blacking out.

His pulse hammered in his ears as he raised his hand to the side of his face, feeling the lump next to his eye. He pulled his hand back, gauging the amount of blood on his fingers. Minimal. He'd live, but whoever had taken a club to him had done a bang-up job.

A degree at a time, the events of the morning came back to him until terror ran through his veins, chased by panic.

He'd taken Rory. The SOB had her again.

"Rory!" he yelled. "Rory!"

He listened for a response.

Nothing.

Anger and fear twisted together in his gut. Somehow, the killer had found them. He'd failed her again.

Logan fought a powerful burst of rage that threatened to tear him apart. He couldn't lose her.

The trail was still warm. He guessed he'd been out for less than an hour. How far could they get?

Scanning the ground with his good eye, he spotted her backpack and knelt next to it. Had the killer taken the walkie-talkie? Or worse. He patted his holster. His pistol was gone.

Caution hitched to his nerves. He was injured and unarmed. No doubt the killer had left him for dead.

He slid the zipper and dug into the pack, locking his hand around the device. If he could contact Sparks again, he could warn him and get help.

Logan turned the dial, bringing the gadget to life. He pressed the talk button. "Anyone out there? This is Sheriff Logan Brewer. I'm stranded below the north face of Reaper's Point. Rory Matson has been abducted. Do you copy?"

Dead silence.

Again, he repeated the location and circumstances.

Nothing.

Had the search been called off? Frustrated, he grabbed the backpack to shove the walkie-talkie back inside, but he grabbed the wrong end. The contents spilled out onto the ground at his feet.

"Dammit." Logan dropped to his knees, feeling utterly defeated.

Rummaging through the mix of stuff, he paused when he picked up the crude map they'd found at the cabin. An instant of hope stirred in his mind as he studied the abstract drawing. Had Dr. Matson really stumbled onto the killer's hiding place? Did either one of the *X*'s represent that location?

Hell, things couldn't get any worse. Before the thought had time to solidify, Logan watched the first snowflake land on his sleeve, then another.

Worry coated his nerves. The trail would vanish once the storm intensified. He shoved the map into his pocket, raked everything up and stuffed it back into the pack, before standing up.

Determination drove him forward as he studied the ground around him, a bloodhound on a scent. Discernable footprints were visible and moving east—toward the Bailey Creek drainage?

Logan hobbled forward, his injured leg throbbing. His body stiff from the cold, his eyesight less than twenty-twenty, but the fire in his blood wouldn't be extinguished. He knew it now. Knew it deep down in his soul.

He was in love with Aurora Matson and nothing was going to keep him from finding her this time.

Nothing.

RORY TURNED AWAY from the horrific sight around her and the lingering stench of old death.

She closed her eyes, but the image of Logan laying on the ground—bloody and beaten to death—was more than she could bear. She'd tried to stop the attack, but he'd broken her arm with a single blow and the struggle had ended. She couldn't even identify the bastard through his full-face ski mask.

The only thing she knew for sure was that Logan wouldn't be coming for her.

Ever.

A sob built in her throat, but she choked it back. She was alone. Utterly and desperately alone. But was she helpless?

She opened her eyes, staring into the half light that pushed into the deep cavern where her abductor had dragged her, tied her up and left her.

They'd only spent half an hour getting to it. It had to be one of the *X*'s her father had drawn in his map of the Bailey Creek drainage.

Struggling to sweep her tied legs underneath her, she tried to come up to a sitting position on the hard dirt floor of the cave, but she couldn't get any leverage with her hands tied in front of her. Her broken arm felt like it was on fire every time she moved.

In desperation, she flopped onto her back. Raising her head, she studied the interior of the cavern. It extended fifty feet back into the mountainside. The entrance was concealed by a pile of rocks and underbrush. She even bet she'd hiked past it before, totally unaware of its existence.

The killer had found the perfect place to hide his victims, several of which, she could just make out in the scant lighting.

How long they'd been here was hard to tell, but one set of remains was missing a femur bone. Probably the bone her father had brought down off of the mountain and concealed in his safe.

Rory let her head drop back before her neck muscles cramped. Was this where he'd taken her? Was this the pit where he'd preformed his sick ritual on her body? Made her touch him?

The thought made her stomach squeeze, as fear pushed through her, raising her heart rate until it pounded in her eardrums.

It would happen all over again if she didn't do something. She had to escape. Raising up again, she searched for anything she could use.

Piles of rock dotted the floor of the cave. If she could find a shard sharp enough, she could saw through the rope on her hands.

Rory rolled onto her side, keeping her broken arm on the up side. She bent her knees, ground her feet into the dirt and pushed off. Repeating the motion, she edged closer to the pile of rock, until she lay next to it, exhausted, her arm throbbing.

There were worse things than a broken arm. Biting back the cry in her throat she rolled onto the rock pile, feeling the sharp edges of the granite cut into her flesh, through her clothing.

Fighting the pain, she fumbled for a shard with enough of an edge to do the job before her masked abductor returned.

Her fingers raked across a particularly sharp rock and she closed her hand around it.

"You can try," her abductor whispered from somewhere in the darkness. "But it won't help. I'm going to have you, Rory, you're my number-one girl and you won't get away this time. Logan can't help you. I made sure of that."

Rory froze. Terror ignited her nerve endings.

She knew his voice.

Realization shot through her reducing her emotions to dust. Logan was dead. There was no one coming.

Ever.

"You bastard!" Swallowing the fear that threatened to close her throat, she felt his hands on her as he pulled her up off of the rocks and yanked her to her feet.

Pain burned through her broken arm, but she gritted her teeth and stared into Deputy Wade Sparks's face, unflinching.

"I've waited a long time for this, Rory. For you to come back to Reaper's Point. Killing your old man expedited it. Too bad I didn't do it years ago, but then, he hadn't found my secret stash yet. He came in here like some sort of hero and took my bones."

He pulled off his right glove and reached for her, stroking his fingers against her cheek.

Rory's stomach lurched.

He closed his eyes, sucking in a deep breath.

She had to keep it together. This was how it had started before. With some sort of sick ritualistic act that he needed to feel powerful. In control. But she'd been blindfolded then, unable to see or read his reactions.

Fear squeezed inside her chest as he opened his eyes and a devious smile split his lips. "I've come a long way since then. You were the first. I bumbled. But I've perfected my methods. It won't take long this time."

Panic zapped through her.

He stepped closer and pulled a blindfold out of his coat pocket. "No man will want you when I'm finished. When you've done the things I'm going to make you do. You're tainted. Do you hear me? I'm going to make you wish you were dead. And then you will be."

His carbon-copy words rattled her resolve. The tape would come next and her screams would be silenced forever.

"What about the girls in L.A.? You killed them, didn't you?"

"Yeah. I was there, working in your lab. So close to you I could smell you, feel your hands on me again. But the timing wasn't right for our second chance, so I took them instead. They died without a fight."

Anger took a hold of her. "I saw you launch off the north face."

"Shock value. You saw what I wanted you to see. I was never in trouble, but how does it make you feel to have saved your killer's life?"

Uncontrollable fear shook her. "Why, Sparks? Just tell me why?"

His eyes glazed over, his face contorted until he was unrecognizable. An odd laugh gurgled in his throat, low at first, until it built to a pitch that put a shiver in her blood. He was crazy. A psychopathic serial killer.

As quick as it had started, it stopped.

The silence was horrible. It ground against her nerves and knifed into her mind.

He stepped up next to her, an angry grimace on his face. "Don't call me Sparks. Wade Sparks is dead. We killed him three years ago."

Caution coated her nerves as she stared into his face, still clutching the sharp rock in her hand. "Then, who are you?"

In one quick movement he covered her eyes with the blindfold and yanked it tight.

Rory's breath caught in her throat.

He grabbed her by the forearm and dragged her to the back of the cave.

LOGAN HUDDLED next to a cluster of trees to catch his breath. The storm's intensity had escalated, a sure sign there would be no help coming.

Digging into his front pocket he fingered the crude map and pulled it out. A hot pink Post-it note was stuck to the map. It was Rory's message from this morning. He'd forgotten to give it to her.

Pulling it closer to his face, he studied the words. It was from her colleague at the lab in L.A., telling her the bones they'd shipped to him four days ago had never arrived.

Caution inched along his nerves as he clutched the paper in his frozen fingers.

He swallowed against the creeping knowledge working its way through to his brain, until his gut fisted.

Deputy Sparks had been in charge of shipping the bones. He had access to the equipment and inside information on every aspect of Rory's case. He'd been on the other end of the walkie-talkie conversation that had pinpointed their location on the mountain. That's what Dr. Matson had stumbled onto.

That's why Matson had to die.

A blade of terror sliced into him. The man he'd considered a fine deputy and a friend was a killer.

Logan hung his head considering the horrific information.

He shoved the Post-it back into his pocket and stared at the map. From his position at the base of the draw, he studied the landmarks against the *X*'s on the map. The snow made it harder to see, but there where two distinct piles of rock that coordinated with the marks on the paper. Did the rocks conceal openings in the granite?

There was only one way to find out.

Logan pulled Rory's pack from his shoulder and unzipped it, pulling out the walkie-talkie.

He waded into the undergrowth and crouched in the brush.

Pressing the signal button several times, he waited for a response.

Nothing.

He held down the talk button. "Sparks, are you out there? Sparks, can you hear me? It's Logan. I'm injured. Rory's been taken. I need your help. Do you copy?"

Tension wound around his spine as he waited for Sparks to take the bait.

"Logan, I copy. What's your twenty?"

Caution laced through him. Sparks was dangerous, and he was unarmed.

"I don't know, I'm disoriented...let me see." Logan hesitated. "I'm west of the north face, trying to get over to the Base-Camp lot trail. We should be able to intersect there."

"Copy that. I'm on my way. Stay put."

"Ten-four." Logan shut off the walkie-talkie and went still, watching the draw for movement.

Through the obscuring of snow, something caught his attention. Focusing intently on it, he could just make out the image of a person making his way down through the rocks. He'd come from behind one of the rock piles. One of Dr. Matson's *X*'s.

Logan dared to hope that Rory was behind that mound of rock, still alive. That he'd been given a second chance.

He watched Sparks's descent until he reached the trail below the clump of brush.

His own breathing sounded like a hurricane in his ears, his heart pounding as he watched Wade move down the trail and break into a jog, a hunting rifle over his shoulder and a pistol on his belt.

Patience. He didn't move until Sparks was out of sight. Reaching down he picked up a thick limb from the ground next to him and crept out of the bushes, careful to stay in the timberline along the trail just in case Sparks came back.

Logan paused. The trail up into the gulch wasn't going to provide much cover. He'd have to hurry, but his damn leg was going to slow him down.

Determination surged in his blood stream. If he stayed low and darted among the rocks and patches of brush, he could make it.

Cautiously, he stepped out from behind a pine tree, staring in the direction Sparks had taken.

All clear.

Logan lunged forward, gritting his teeth against the pain burning in his body.

Fifty feet, he ducked behind a tall patch of buck brush and pulled in a breath. Keeping his focus on the rocks above, he took off again, covering the terrain in long even strides. He couldn't give up. He had to get to her.

He reached a pile of rock and slipped in next to it, his body throbbing, his lungs on fire.

Was he too late? Had Sparks already killed her?

Biting back the curse on his tongue, he stepped out again. Anger and frustration driving him forward.

The first bullet caught him in the back, hammering into his body armor like a sledge.

The second bullet whizzed past his ear and bore into the tree directly in front of him.

Logan hit the ground, his muscles on fire, his thoughts racing.

Crawling on his belly he pulled up behind a massive tree trunk.

Dammit. Sparks must have figured out his ruse. And now he would kill him in short order if he didn't come up with a plan.

The rock pile Sparks had emerged from behind was only twenty-five feet away. But it was a naked twenty-five feet with no cover.

The shot had come from the rifle. Sparks could get off a 350-yard shot.

Logan studied the lay of the ground. He was on a steep uphill slope.

Pulling off his coat, he raised himself up, careful to stay concealed behind the tree.

A sucker branch poked out of the trunk at chest level.

Logan turned his coat, letting one of the sleeves flop out.

Pop!

A bullet tore through the sleeve. Logan pulled it back, letting out a yell of pain.

His thinking was right. Sparks had taken a bead on the tree, waiting for any sort of movement.

Raising the jacket he thrust it against the branch. On the third try the stick tore through the fabric, holding the jacket in place on the tree.

Logan swallowed, praying his plan would work.

He went to his knees, then carefully let the jacket sleeve drop. If Sparks wanted a target, he'd give him one.

Carefully, he flattened himself on the ground and slid out from behind the tree on his belly.

A shot went off. He heard it pucker the fabric of the coat. Then another.

Crawling like his life depended on it, he moved away from the tree, his focus on the rocks above him.

He was counting on Sparks's focus being on the jacket sleeve and not on his getaway. The view through the rifle scope was limited. Just another minute and he'd be clear.

Like a soldier on a mission he scurried over the rough ground. Rocks and sticks bit into his flesh. He wouldn't give up. He'd never give up.

Ten feet.

Pop! A bullet bit into the ground next to him, sending splinters of rock and soil up around him.

He kept moving, never taking his eyes off the pile of granite in front of him.

Pop! The bullet glanced the back of his thigh sending white-hot pain through his leg. He kept moving.

Five feet…four feet…three feet…

Logan pushed hard, diving behind the mound of rock. He rolled onto his back, staring up at a black hole. The opening to a cave. Tension knotted his nerves and settled in his gut. He swallowed and sat up, careful to stay lower than the top of the rock pile.

Sparks was out there and coming fast.

The clock in his head ticked off the seconds before the madman reached him.

Logan came to his feet, but stayed hunched over. Pushing into the dark cave.

Bracing, he listened. Nothing but the wind outside. Stepping farther inside, he tried to make out the interior of the cavern with his limited sight.

A flash of movement on his right set his nerves on edge.

He whirled toward the shadowy figure as it hit him full force, knocking him backward.

Pain knifed into his chest, but he managed to stay on his feet.

"Rory!" he yelled, trying to gain control of the situation. "Rory. It's me."

With his arms around her, he pulled her close, feeling her shudder.

"I thought you were dead."

"Not a chance. Not this time, but we've got to hurry. Sparks is headed this way. He took my gun."

"Mine, too."

Logan squeezed the limb in his hand. "We're going to have to do this together." He tried to gauge her reaction with his good eye, but he couldn't see her clear enough in the dimness of the cavern.

"An ambush is the only way. If we can get him into the opening, I'll take him out with this." He indicated the limb. It was thick enough, but the timing would have to be perfect.

"You're going to have to grab his gun and shoot him. We'll have one chance. You can't miss." Raising his hand he touched her cheek and felt her tears.

"Let's do it." Rory pulled away from Logan. Their odds of getting off the mountain minus a body bag were minimal at best, but courage surged in her veins. Logan was here. He'd come for her this time.

Pushing backward she watched him back up against the wall next to the opening.

She pushed back into the darkness, blending

with the stone, mentally preparing for what would come next. Could she kill another human being?

Could she pull the trigger and watch him die?

Yes, she decided as she watched the entrance, fear and anticipation circling in her system, tying her in knots.

It was either kill or be killed.

Chapter Fourteen

Logan trained his limited line of sight on the narrow opening.

Sparks would come in shooting.

They had one chance to take him out.

The wind whistled outside, driving the snow in white swirls.

The hair at Logan's nape stood up as he watched a shape take form and materialize out of the storm.

Holding his breath, he counted the seconds, waiting until Sparks stepped inside the opening.

With all the force he could muster, he swung the club.

The wood made contact with the back of Sparks's neck.

Sparks lurched forward and swung around.

The barrel of the rifle pointed in Logan's direction.

Logan brought the club down on the gun barrel.

It dislodged from Sparks's grasp.

Sparks bellowed, his words incomprehensible.

No mercy.

He brought the stick down again, making contact with Sparks's broken ribs.

Where was Rory? Why hadn't she taken Sparks's gun?

Panic raced through him as he tried to assess the situation within his limited visual field.

The rifle wasn't his only weapon. He had a side arm. "Get the rifle, Rory!" Caution surged inside of him.

She lunged out of the shadows.

He heard the clash of physical contact, then gunfire.

Two shots echoed against the walls of the cave.

His ears rang.

He froze. Trying to reconcile the fear knotting his gut.

The only thing he could make out were two shapes, intertwined in the shadows.

Rory and Sparks.

Slowly, one melted away from the other.

Logan stepped forward, unsure who'd gone to the ground. Prepared to do battle.

"Rory?"

"Yeah?"

Relief pulsed in his veins as he stepped toward her and pulled her into his arms. "Thank God."

He held her tightly, feeling her shudder again and again. A release of emotion he understood.

"It'll be okay. Sparks is dead. He won't ever hurt you again."

She pulled back and he focused on her face. "He's not Wade Sparks. He said he killed Sparks three years ago."

"If he's not Sparks, then, who in the hell is he?"

"He's my brother."

The voice from the cave opening startled them both.

Logan moved Rory behind him. Caution sizzled along his fried nerves.

"Relax, Brewer." Brady Morris moved into the cave and shined a flashlight beam on his brother's body. "Teddy was never right in the head. Even when we were kids. Our overbearing mother belittled him nonstop. He hated her. So did I. I realize now I should have turned him in years ago, after he escaped from the institution, but I couldn't. He's my flesh and blood. I planted the bones on Reaper's Ledge to get your attention."

"He's a serial killer. Six women suffered and died because of him." Logan studied the look of regret that flashed across Brady's face. It seemed genuine.

A measure of uneasiness slid up his spine. Why would Brady protect a killer? Blood was thick, but there was something twisted about the level of dedication.

"Do you have a radio?" Logan asked, stepping closer to Sparks's body.

"Yes." Morris moved closer.

The air in the cave vibrated with tension. Charged particles of malice unseen, but deadly if ignored. A warning screamed inside Logan's brain.

Who was protecting who? Was the man laying dead on the dirt really the killer?

Caution raced over his nerves as they squared off in the dim light. Where was the rifle? Trying to focus, Logan glanced at the ground, seeing the long gun on the floor at his feet.

"Why don't you radio for help? We need to get Rory out of here."

"Help won't be coming, Brewer. This ends here. Teddy is dead and so is his fascination with killing young women. I told him to get rid of those damn boots and I assume he did. There's nothing to link him in any way to the crimes except you two. I can't let you live. It's over."

"Is it? I think you're as much a part of it as he was. And what about the real Wade Sparks?"

Rage glistened in Brady's eyes for an instant. "Wade Sparks died so Teddy could live. When he escaped from the institution he came here and hid on the mountain, but being stuck up here made him worse. I told him to stop killing those girls, but he wouldn't listen. That's when I met Sparks on a climb three years ago and realized how much he and Teddy looked alike. We killed him and gave his identity to Ted."

"That makes you a murderer."

"I'm my brother's keeper, you bastard." Brady gave a guttural yell and lunged forward.

Logan ducked, taking the force like a football player in a tackle. He rammed Brady and rolled him over his shoulder.

Reaching down, he snagged the rifle, pulled it up into firing position and whirled around, focusing the red laser dot on Brady's chest.

Horror sliced into him as he took stock of the situation.

The marker from the rifle wasn't focused on Brady. It was lined up on Rory.

"I wouldn't," Brady said, holding a long bladed knife at Rory's throat.

"Unless you want her to bleed out in front of you. Put the gun down."

"Shoot, Logan! Kill him."

A moment of indecision froze the blood in his veins.

In a split-second decision, he drew the red dot up onto Brady's forehead and pulled the trigger.

The bullet sliced through the air and ripped into Brady Morris.

Logan bolted forward, his ears ringing from the blast.

Rory stumbled into his arms. He pulled her toward the mouth of the cavern, stopping in the opening where he could check her over. "Are you okay? Are you hit?"

"I'm fine. Thank God, you took the shot. He

was going to kill me." Her hand went to her throat where a long gash started to bleed. "They're both psycho," she whispered, glancing toward the inside of the cave.

Logan dropped the rifle and slid down the rock, taking her with him, until they were seated on the ground.

"Take it easy. We don't know how deep that wound goes. I don't want to lose you, Rory. Not now…not ever. We'll use Brady's two-way radio to get help."

Her hand closed around his arm, her fingers digging into his flesh. "I love you, Logan. I always have, I just didn't have the sense to realize it."

Focusing on her face, he reached up to stroke her cheek and watched her smile. "Does that mean you're going to stay in Reaper's Point? Because I can't live without you anymore."

"Yeah. I'm going to stay." Rory leaned into Logan, feeling him shiver. Was his virile body reacting to the cold or the emotional tension? She wasn't sure. But one fact couldn't be disputed. She loved him.

Pulling back she smiled up into his face, but grimaced when she checked out his swollen eye and battered head.

"You took a hell of a beating for me. I thought you were dead, but when I heard your voice come over the walkie-talkie…" Her heart squeezed in her chest, her throat closing with emotion.

"I got a second chance and I'd have taken as many beatings as I had to in order to get you back."

"Make that radio call and let's get off this mountain." She came to her feet and reached down to help him up, noting that the snow was diminishing. The storm was passing.

This was her mountain again, she decided as she listened to Logan give their location.

The killer's control over her life was finished.

Together they stood in the mouth of the cavern holding onto each other.

"Will you stay, Rory?" Logan had to hear the words again.

She looked up at him and smiled. "There's no where else I want to be. I love you, Logan. And I love this mountain."

His lowered his mouth to hers, kissing her until heat flooded her body.

Reaper's Point belonged to them once more.

Epilogue

Logan signed his name to the last report on the Morris brothers' case and closed the folder.

It had taken six months to pull it all together into a cohesive case file and he was sure there were things they would never know about the twisted siblings. The Brothers Psycho, as Rory liked to call them.

Ted Morris had always been a troubled young man, a sickness his parents had tried to cover up with money, but Ted had every characteristic of a serial killer. His mother's overbearing personality had probably set him off.

Two sets of remains were found in the cave. Victims three and six, according to the marks on their foreheads, had been identified as twenty-three-year-old Leslie Nolan and twenty-seven-year-old Jennifer Benz. Both girls had set off to hike Reaper's Point, four years apart, but neither one made it off the mountain alive. Victim seven was

Ann Jenkins, a twenty-one-year-old waitress from Cliff Side.

Logan's heart squeezed. If only they'd have caught Ted Morris sooner… But he'd been good at his act. Hell, he'd even been bold enough to use Wade Sparks's exemplary military record to get into the department. Providing a fingerprint card with Sparks's prints as his own. Logan still hadn't figured out how he'd pulled it off. Maybe he never would.

The real Wade Sparks's remains had been located in a cave above the one where the brothers had died, but he'd been unable to locate any family members to date.

Everything had been orchestrated by Ted Morris. He'd tried to abduct Rory from the condo. He'd committed arson so he could plant the pressure bomb, hoping to blow Logan out of the picture and take away Rory's protection. And he'd cut the brake lines on the Blazer and broke into the cabin, hoping to destroy the secrets Dr. Matson had discovered.

Logan looked up from behind the stack of paperwork on his desk and smiled at his wife as she stood in the doorway, her arms crossed over her expanding middle.

Their child was tucked safely away awaiting his upcoming due date.

He smiled, remembering how close he'd come to losing her.

"You're looking sexy today, Mrs. Brewer." He stood up.

Rory glared at him and glanced over her shoulder. "Shh." She stepped into the office. "Someone might hear you."

Logan grabbed his hat off the corner of the desk and slapped it on his head. "Let them hear. I'd shout it from the top of the mountain if you'd let me."

"You're a nut. It's time to get going."

"Are you sure you're up to this?"

"Give me a break. I'm pregnant, not in a wheelchair. I can hack it, Brewer. Besides, we're not going all the way."

He moved in on her, wanting to feel her body next to his with a hunger that devoured him almost every waking second of the day.

Reaching down he rested his hand on her belly.

In response, the baby moved, pushing against the pressure.

"I can hardly wait to see you, little one," he whispered. "Your dad would be proud," Logan said as he straightened. Looking into Rory's eyes, he noted a single tear as it rolled down her cheek.

He brushed it away. "You're sure?"

"Yeah."

"We could wait until after the baby comes. Your dad would understand."

"I've waited long enough."

"I have something for you." Logan picked up the plastic evidence bag from his desk and opened it.

"We recovered it in the search at Ted Morris's place. It's been released from evidence."

A small but audible gasp left Rory's lips and his heart squeezed.

"My necklace."

"Yeah."

She turned her back to him as he straightened the chain and slipped the trinket around her neck before closing the clasp.

He pulled her against him and kissed the top of her head. It was finished.

"Thank you," she whispered, laying her hand over the cross at the end of the chain.

"You're welcome."

Taking her hand they left the office and walked outside.

The sun was high in the sky, the air brisk, but warming with the promise of summer. Green tinted the leaves on the trees. There was hope in the air.

Together they stared at the snowcapped mountain.

"It's where he wanted to be," Rory whispered.

"So what are we waiting for?" They strolled to the car and climbed in for the drive up the mountain to scatter her father's ashes in the place he'd loved.

It was fitting that he would forever inhabit the mountain and fitting that his grandchild would soon take his first breath in the world.

Life went on.

"I love you, Logan," Rory whispered from the seat next to his as she took his hand in hers.

She'd returned to Reaper's Point and reluctantly conquered her fear with his help and his protection. Because of it, she was safe again.

Contentment stirred in her veins as Logan put the car in gear and headed for the mountain.

She liked new beginnings…especially when they came with a badge and a Stetson.

* * * * *

*Mills & Boon® Intrigue brings you a sneak
preview of Caridad Piñeiro's*
Secret Agent Reunion…

*A mysterious betrayal led super spy Danielle
Moore to fake her own death. Now she is ready
to re-emerge and seek vengeance. But things
get complicated when she realises a mole in her
agency is still leaking vital information – and her
new partner is an ex-lover she thought was dead.*

*Don't miss the fantastic second story
in the thrilling*
MISSION: IMPASSIONED
*series, available next month in
Mills & Boon® Intrigue!*

Secret Agent Reunion
by
Caridad Piñeiro

Only someone who had come back from the dead truly knew how deadly distractions could be.

Danielle Moore had let personal feelings get in the way of a top-secret mission over a year ago and had nearly lost her life. So she kept her eyes glued to the man—six feet two inches of thick muscle—as he charged at her like a linebacker after a quarterback, arms outstretched to trap her in his embrace.

Dani used his momentum against him, sweeping him aside with a matador like step. Turning quickly as he stumbled by, she snapped an elbow to the back of his neck and dropped him to the ground. Before she could totally incapacitate him, another more compact man charged at her from the opposite side of the room.

She pushed off the first man's fallen body and came up ready for action, but as she did so, something pulled along her midsection. A twinge of pain followed, but she tamped it down. She couldn't allow physical discomfort or weakness to divert her attention.

As the smaller man shoved past his rising friend, she released a sharp dropkick, catching him squarely in the chest and rocking him backward, where he immediately tripped over the larger man. Both men sprawled to the ground in a messy heap.

Dani stopped, placed her hands on her hips and laughed as they tried to untangle themselves and resume their attack.

"Come on, boys. Is that the best you can do?" she teased in fluent French.

After months of training together, the three of them had developed an easy camaraderie. Even now, when the men couldn't seem to contain Dani as her physical strength and martial arts prowess returned rapidly, they accepted her superior abilities good-naturedly.

Her current physical state was quite different from what it had been nearly three months ago, Dani thought.

After being shot and lingering in a coma off and on, she had emerged long enough to approve the removal of the bullet that had lodged precariously close to her spine. Three months after that, she had finally been well enough to begin physical therapy and try to get back into shape.

She had a new mission waiting for her, after all. At least, that's what the enigmatic man by her bedside had intimated to her so many months ago.

Dani now knew who that mysterious angel was—Corbett Lazlo, the elusive powerhouse behind the Lazlo Group, a private agency known for handling the most discreet and sometimes dangerous of missions. A group well known to her from her time with the Secret Intelligence Service, or SIS, the British equivalent of the CIA and the agency at which she had worked as the Sparrow, a world-renowned assassin.

Only she hadn't really been an assassin. All her supposed "kills" had been taken into SIS custody so that SIS might find out more information about an elusive crime organization they called SNAKE, which they suspected of being responsible for a number of illegal operations.

She had let her last mission get personal. Her actions had resulted in the death of the prince of Silvershire and had nearly caused her death and that of her twin sister. SIS had been less than pleased that, in her quest to find her parents' killers, she had messed up the mission in Silvershire, the small European island kingdom she had called home at one time. With her cover as the Sparrow possibly blown and an international incident brewing, SIS had tossed her out.

Lazlo, who had also been thrown out of SIS many years earlier, was the man she had to thank for keeping her alive. He was the one responsible for the medical treatment that had worked a miracle and brought her back from the dead.

He had taken her into his agency and told her that he would let her know when the time was right for her to be reborn and go out on another mission.

She felt mission-ready now and sensed that somehow Lazlo would know that.

He seemed to know everything about everyone while she, like most of the people she had met within his group, knew little about him. To her surprise, few had even seen the elusive Mr. Lazlo.

After thanking her two sparring partners for the training session, she walked to the gym to finish her workout. She took a place at the first station and lifted the weights, evenly pushing up the bars on the bench press and enjoying the strength she had regained in her arms. Satisfied, she finished her reps and moved on to the next station and then the next.

By the time she finished, her muscles trembled from her exertions, but it was a good feeling. The kind of sore that said she was getting stronger.

The kind of pain that confirmed she was still alive.

In the locker room, she peeled off her clothes and grabbed a towel, ready for a long soak in the Jacuzzi. As she passed a mirror, she stopped short, surprised by what stared back at her.

The image of a hard-bodied woman of average height was reflected in the mirror. Shoulder-length hair in need of a trim. Fine-boned shoulders leading to full breasts above a long, barely pink scar that ran down her middle. Beside the scar was the ragged, stellar-shaped wound where she had been shot during her last mission.

The physical wounds of the past year were alive in her vision, much like those in her heart, which had been there far longer. The scar of her parents' murder. The ragged and still unhealed wound from her lover's death barely three years ago.

Dani ran her hand down the long scar, but it was numb. Just as she was numb inside. Paralyzed. Yet she still had things to do so that might make her feel alive again.

So that she could finally go home. Go and see her twin sister, Elizabeth.

Only, as she'd heard before, she suspected that she could never truly go home again.

Lazlo agent Mitch Lama watched as Dani sparred with the two men in the gym.

Was she ready? he wondered tapping his lips with his index finger as Dani deftly handled the two much larger men.

The frailness from her injuries was gone, as was the pallor that had colored her skin for the many months she had been unconscious and battling for life. Months during which he had come to sit by her bedside, urging her to keep up the fight. Reading to her in hopes that she might hear his voice and return because they had things to settle between them.

Now she was back from the dead and he didn't know what to do with her. What to do about the lies she had told him for so long. Lies that had nearly cost him his life and hers.

She looked strong now. Presumably ready for action.

He had always admired Dani's physicality. Been intrigued by the strength beneath the seemingly fragile and feminine surface.

She was a warrior. A champion who was forever prepared to take up a cause and fight a wrong.

He both loved and hated her for being a hero.

For nearly three years, he had been waiting to see her. To talk to her again. To be able to touch her and have her know it was him.

To ask her why she had lied to him about who she was, even as he'd lain dying.

A loud beep came from his computer, notifying him that he had an urgent message from Corbett Lazlo. A second later, his phone rang and he had no doubt who would be on the line.

He shut down his access to the camera trained on Dani, immediately regretting the loss of her.

"Lama," he said, a tinge of annoyance in his voice that he had been pulled away from his surveillance.

Corbett Lazlo identified himself. "Did you get my message?"

"Hold on just one second, sir, while I open it," he said, the cadence and tone from his days in the military coloring his speech. He double-clicked to open the e-mail message Lazlo had forwarded and held his breath as he read it.

The message threatened with its simplicity.

Ready for Round 2?

"I'm assuming Cordez couldn't track the source of this message either?" He wondered why their top computer person was having such difficulty tracing the mysterious missives.

"You're correct. Plus, I have some other news."

He knew the news would be bad so he preempted Lazlo's report. "Another operative is down. I'm assuming the same MO as before?"

"Unfortunately, yes. His body was discovered not far from our Prague offices. Close-range shot to the head, just above the left ear. Hollow-point bullet. I've asked our various contacts to see if they have a record of any assassins with a similar MO but I suspect there may be quite a few."

Mitch considered the facts and sensed that the moment for waiting and watching had ended. Time for him and the Sparrow to join forces and discover who was behind the messages and attacks.

"I'm assuming that you want me to activate the Lazarus Liaison now, Mr. Lazlo."

Silence came across the line before Lazlo asked, "Do you think she's ready?"

He recalled the sight of Dani as she sparred. "I think she's physically ready, sir."

"Quite the political answer. And you? Are you ready? Physically? Emotionally?"

He'd be a liar if he said "yes," and so he provided the only answer he could.

"That remains to be seen, sir."

Celebrate 100 years of pure reading pleasure with Mills & Boon®

To mark our centenary, each month we're publishing a special 100th Birthday Edition. These celebratory editions are packed with extra features and include a FREE bonus story.

Plus, you have the chance to enter a fabulous monthly prize draw. See 100th Birthday Edition books for details.

Now that's worth celebrating!

July 2008

The Man Who Had Everything by Christine Rimmer
Includes FREE bonus story *Marrying Molly*

August 2008

Their Miracle Baby by Caroline Anderson
Includes FREE bonus story *Making Memories*

September 2008

Crazy About Her Spanish Boss by Rebecca Winters
Includes FREE bonus story
Rafael's Convenient Proposal

Look for Mills & Boon® 100th Birthday Editions at your favourite bookseller or visit
www.millsandboon.co.uk

FREE

4 BOOKS AND A SURPRISE GIFT!

We would like to take this opportunity to thank you for reading this Mills & Boon® book by offering you the chance to take FOUR more specially selected titles from the Intrigue series absolutely FREE! We're also making this offer to introduce you to the benefits of the Mills & Boon® Book Club™—

- ★ **FREE home delivery**
- ★ **FREE gifts and competitions**
- ★ **FREE monthly Newsletter**
- ★ **Books available before they're in the shops**
- ★ **Exclusive Mills & Boon Book Club offers**

Accepting these FREE books and gift places you under no obligation to buy; you may cancel at any time, even after receiving your free shipment. Simply complete your details below and return the entire page to the address below. You don't even need a stamp!

YES! Please send me 4 free Intrigue books and a surprise gift. I understand that unless you hear from me, I will receive 6 superb new titles every month for just £3.15 each, postage and packing free. I am under no obligation to purchase any books and may cancel my subscription at any time. The free books and gift will be mine to keep in any case.

I8ZEE

Ms/Mrs/Miss/Mr...Initials ....
BLOCK CAPITALS PLEASE

Surname ....

Address ....

....

....Postcode ....

Send this whole page to:

The Mills & Boon Book Club, FREEPOST CN81, Croydon, CR9 3WZ